Readers Love ANDREW GREY

Heartward

"For something quick, light, and bright, I can honestly recommend *Heartward*."

—Rainbow Book Reviews

Only the Brightest Stars

"If you love Andrew Grey's work, pick this one up. It's a decent story with a HEA ending that satisfies."

—Sparkling Book Reviews

In the Weeds

"Another solid, feel-good story that is perfect for coffee-time or to wind down at the end of the day."

—Love Bytes Reviews

Rescue Me

"This was a beautiful story of overcoming abuse, of two men who each want to be in a loving relationship and have to put the past in the past."

—Paranormal Romance Guild

By Andrew Grey

Published by Dreamspinner Press
www.dreamspinnerpress.com

By ANDREW GREY (cont'd)

Published by DREAMSPINNER PRESS
www.dreamspinnerpress.com

By ANDREW GREY (cont'd)

Published by DREAMSPINNER PRESS
www.dreamspinnerpress.com

ANDREW GREY

HOMEWARD

DREAMSPINNER
PRESS

Published by
DREAMSPINNER PRESS

8219 Woodville Hwy #1245
Woodville, FL 32362 USA
www.dreamspinnerpress.com

Homeward
© 2024 Andrew Grey

Cover Art
© 2024 L.C. Chase
http://www.lcchase.com
Cover content is for illustrative purposes only and any person depicted on the cover is a model.

Trade Paperback ISBN: 978-1-64108-658-5
Digital ISBN: 978-1-64108-657-8
Trade Paperback published May 2024
v. 1.0

To Karen R. and Dominic for all their support and love.

CHAPTER 1

"CUT," BARRY called, and Lucas Reardon broke character and smiled as he strode off set. "That was amazing, and we got what we need here. Let's set up for the final interior apartment shots."

Once he had given his instructions, Barry, the director of the much-anticipated film Lucas was starring in, walked to where Lucas sat. "We should wrap this tomorrow, on schedule."

"I appreciate that." Filming had been running behind because of weather on location, but now that they had moved indoors, Barry had lengthened the filming days and they'd made up for lost time. Lucas only had two weeks before he was scheduled to be on set for another film, and he had been hoping for some time off. Not that he would be spending it in Tahiti or anything. He still had publicity to do for the movie releasing next month. Sometimes it seemed like he was on a treadmill, except he wasn't walking on it—he was the motor keeping the whole thing going. "If you don't need me, I'm going home for a while."

"Stay in your trailer. I'll put someone outside to make sure you aren't disturbed. We need to start at six in the morning."

Lucas nodded. "Will my two scenes be first?" God, he hoped so.

"Yes. We'll shoot the last things we need from you, and then you can go." Barry smiled, which was a rarity for him. "You are going to be so amazing in this, and working with you is a dream." He shifted his gaze to where Henry West and Vanessa Ritter stood talking to each other like a couple of chickens hatching their next plot to steal a rival's eggs. They had married eighteen months ago and seemed to feed on each other's prima-donna energy.

"Thank you," Lucas said as he followed Barry's gaze. "Never again… with either of them." He met Barry's gaze and received a nod of solidarity in return.

"Get some rest, and I'll see you in the morning." Barry dashed off to deal with his problems, and Lucas made his escape to his trailer, where his assistant waited for him.

Karen Robeson was the best assistant he had ever had. She'd been with him for a year, and Lucas hoped she stayed on. Karen looked up from her tablet, smiling as she got up, opened the refrigerator, and handed him a Diet Coke. He popped it open and drank.

"God."

"What time is your call tomorrow morning?"

"Six. I should be done by eight, so let's have everything ready to go. As soon as I'm done, I want to go home. I'm not taking meetings for at least two days."

"I know the routine," she said as she tapped away. "I've had the cleaners in the house, so it's spotless, and I stocked it today. Everything you like is there. The cars have been washed and detailed, the pool is sparkling, and I even put in an order to make sure the city is extra sparkly at night." She didn't break a smile. Lucas loved her sense of humor. She reached into her bag and pulled out a sheet of paper, which she handed to him.

Lucas opened it. "That little shit," he swore. "Henry tried to steal you away?"

Karen nodded and shivered slightly. "You know I'd never work for them."

"I do." He messaged his business manager to give Karen a thousand-dollar bonus. "And a deal is a deal." He got a thumbs-up response.

"Thanks, Lucas," she said gently and sat back down in her out-of-the-way spot, tapping away and then scowling. "Ummm…. Check your phone."

"Huh?" He never brought it with him on set. It was rude, and more than once a perfectly good take was ruined by someone's damned phone, and it wasn't going to be his. She sighed and went through to the back bedroom area and returned to press it into his hand.

Lucas read the messages from his aunt, which were coming in quickly. Then he set the phone on the counter next to the sink, entered the bedroom area, and pulled the curtain closed. "Fuck," he said, just once, and sat on the edge of the bed.

The trailer was quiet, the only sounds coming from outside, including the clomping of a horse's hooves as it passed. You never knew what to expect on a movie lot. He closed his eyes, shaking his head.

"Lucas, what do you want to do?" Karen asked after a good five minutes.

"I want…," he began, and then he retrieved his phone and called his aunt. She answered on the second ring.

"Auntie Rose," he said quietly, refusing to choke up over an old bastard who had left Lucas and his mother when he fell in love with someone four years older than Lucas was at the time. His dad's second wife had been the student aide in his middle school drama class, for God's sake.

"I know how things are between you and your father. But...." She was the only one on his father's side of the family that he spoke with at all. "Look, I'll be blunt. If you want the chance to make peace with your father, then you need to come home now. Say what you want to say, yell at the old codger, but if you have anything you want to tell him, get on a plane and get here. His days are numbered, and we're talking single digits."

Lucas swallowed hard. He didn't want anything to do with his father, but his aunt was right. If the old asshole was going to die, Lucas needed to be there, say what he wanted, and then see him off on his journey to hell—or at least that's where he hoped cheating assholes who left their wife and son hanging out to dry ended up. "I don't know."

Aunt Rose cleared her throat. "You know he's alone. Cherie is gone. Cancer... a year ago."

"I know. You told me."

"So will you come? Can you come?" The grief hung in her voice, and Lucas knew there was no way he could turn her down. "Make some sort of peace for both of you before he's gone. If nothing else, you'll know you tried."

The timing worked from a job perspective, but Lucas was worn out from weeks of long days and nights of filming, and he needed a chance to rest. It looked like he wasn't going to get it. "Okay. I'll see what I can do and let you know."

"Should I tell your father you're coming?" Aunt Rose asked.

"No," Lucas answered. "I'll let you know what I can work out." He set the phone aside and lay back on the bed, closing his eyes and just trying not to fly into a million little pieces. "Karen?" he said, not moving or opening his eyes.

"I know, Lucas. I'm already looking into flights for you."

"For us," he corrected. "I need you to come with me."

The curtain slid on its rod, and he lifted his head. "You know I can't," she told him. "I'll do whatever you need, but I can't go and leave my brother here alone."

Lucas nodded. "Sorry. I remember now." Karen had a brother in a school for kids with special needs, and Karen looked after him and made sure Lincoln knew he wasn't alone. Lucas admired her for that dedication. "Stay near him."

"What about Jerry?" she asked.

"He's out of town with his new boyfriend." For being a household name throughout much of the country, Lucas had a surprisingly lonely life. "I'll go on my own. I should be fine."

"You will not," Karen snapped, her fingers flying over her tablet. "How about Rachel? She looked after you last year when that stalker business got ugly. She's good, professional, and you liked her. She can stand in as your on-site assistant, and she can provide security if you need it."

"Then call her and make all the arrangements." Rachel was amazing, and she could kick ass. He'd seen it firsthand. Not that he expected trouble in Scottville, Michigan, but backup was always a good thing to have.

Lucas drank some more soda and then lay down and closed his eyes, trying to settle his mind. He was going home, but first he had a movie to finish, and that was where his head needed to be, not three thousand miles away.

"I have your flight all set, as well as a car. Rachel will meet you at your house tomorrow. I got you on a red-eye at ten, and you'll be in Detroit in the morning. From there you fly to Grand Rapids, and Rachel will drive you up to Scottville from there. I've sent messages to your agent and your business manager so they know what's going on. I also messaged Barry's assistant." She placed a tray next to him. "And you need to eat."

"You're a goddess, you know that?" Lucas told her.

"Rest and eat." The door to the trailer opened and closed behind her as she left. Lucas ate what he could, then reviewed the scenes for tomorrow before trying to sleep.

HE HATED planes, especially when he was tired. Lucas could never sleep regardless of how comfortable the seat was or how well his noise-canceling headphones worked. Fortunately, Rachel sat next to him in first class, and he could relax knowing she'd run interference for him.

Airports were another matter entirely, with crowds of people trying to get where they needed. Things got tougher when a lady recognized him just outside the gate in Detroit and decided to scream his name up and down the concourse. Lucas never stopped moving and made it to his connection on time. He settled in his seat, doing his best not to be recognized.

"We're fine now," Rachel said. "The crew is aware and will keep people moving." She was almost as efficient as Karen.

By the time they landed and got in the car, Lucas could barely keep his eyes open. He got as comfortable as he could, put the seat back as far as it would go, and fell asleep, only waking when the sound of the wheels changed. "What happened?"

"The clouds opened up," Rachel said as she continued driving, water everywhere. "Reports are that this continues all the way to our destination. I slowed down, but I want to get off the road as quickly as I can. Go back to sleep if you want. It's going to take a while."

"Thanks." Lucas closed his eyes once more and let exhaustion take over. He was in the best hands possible.

"Sir," Rachel said as they got off the freeway.

"Lucas, please," he said gently.

"Do you want to go to the hotel or right up to the hospital?" Rachel asked.

"My aunt's." He showed her the address on his phone, and she pulled over, entered it into her phone, and then followed the directions through the driving rain.

Things were still largely the same as he remembered. There was the McDonald's where he'd gotten his first job, and the Meijers grocery store. They passed the hospital in Ludington and continued west into town before turning off the main street. Rachel found the house easily, and it seemed just the same too. Basically square, two stories. White with green trim.

The rain let up a little, and Rachel reached into the back seat and retrieved two black umbrellas. He took one and cracked the door, popped the umbrella open, and then got out of the car.

"Do you want me to come?"

"Yes." He wasn't going to ask her to wait in the car. "I have no idea what I'm walking into as far as the family is concerned. If things start to go south, remind me of a meeting with Spielberg and we'll get out of here." That always worked. Poor Steven took more fake meetings than anyone in Hollywood. "If I ask you to postpone my afternoon meeting, then you'll know everything is okay."

"What's your code word?" Rachel asked. "What will you say if I'm to get you out now?"

"Bananas. I hate the danged things, so if I say something nice about them or ask for one, we go now." She nodded, and Lucas hurried to the front door, which opened right away.

"I thought you were going to stand out there talking all day," his aunt said with a smile before ushering him inside. Lucas had barely gotten his umbrella down before he was hugged within an inch of his life. "It's good to see you in real life. I see all your movies." She released him and stepped back. "You look better in person, but you're too skinny."

Rachel came in and closed the door.

"Aunt Rose, this is Rachel."

"I see," she said, narrowing her gaze.

"Aunt Rose, no conclusion jumping. Rachel is here as my assistant and as security."

Aunt Rose shook her head. "She looks like a stiff breeze could blow her away."

Lucas chuckled. "Be nice. I've seen her take down men four times her size and leave them whimpering for their mamas on the sidewalk. She's not someone you want to piss off." He winked at Rachel, and she crossed her arms over her chest, looking even more badass.

"I see. Do you want some tea or coffee?" she asked both of them.

"Coffee for both of us is fine." He'd seen Rachel mainline the stuff. "Then we should go up to see Dad." Get that over with. Then maybe he could head back to the land of sunshine and swimming pools, where movie stars belonged.

Aunt Rose led the way into her bright, warm kitchen. Lucas had spent many hours at the table in this room, eating cookies and brownies as Aunt Rose helped him learn his lines for whatever play or show he could get a part in. She brought them coffee and then sat down across from him. "Your dad is fading fast. When I saw him this morning, he was talking a little, but he's really weak. His liver and kidneys are shutting down, as are other organs." She sipped from her mug, and Lucas bought his own to his lips and sipped the nectar of life with gratitude. "I didn't say anything on the phone, but he's been asking for you."

Lucas sighed. "That's a surprise."

"When you know you're going to meet your maker, you realize what's important." Aunt Rose lifted her gaze to the holy pictures on the wall. "This is a chance for both of you to have a little peace."

"What about the arrangements?"

"They've all been made already. Cremation, a simple service, and then he'll be interred with our parents. There's nothing you need to do." That was Aunt Rose. If they let her, she could run the Pentagon in her spare time. "How long will you be staying?"

Lucas shrugged.

"Karen figured three or four days," Rachel said. "But she left things open for you."

"Then I'll be here for a couple of days or so. I just finished filming and don't start another project for two more weeks."

Aunt Rose clapped her hands once, grinning. "Then you can stay for the children's benefit. We're raising money for a new addition to the hospital for pediatrics. We've been having a hard time selling tickets. It's just a few days, and it could mean so much to the area where you grew up."

Rachel finished her coffee, and Lucas switched mugs with her. "Let me think about it." He looked outside and saw the rain had let up. "Why don't we go to the hospital to see Dad?" he told Rachel. "We passed it on the way here. Then we can check in and I can rest awhile."

"Very good," Rachel said, and they all stood. Lucas hugged his aunt and promised to call her. Then he and Rachel left the house and retraced their steps. When they parked in the hospital lot, the clouds hung low, and it looked like they would open up again at any moment. Lucas went inside and up to the visitors' desk. "Adam Reardon," he told the lady.

She looked up at him. "Only family members are allowed."

"I'm his son," Lucas said, and she lifted her gaze. He realized the moment she recognized him. To her credit, she didn't yell, but she did smile brightly.

"And this lady?" she asked.

Lucas leaned forward. "She's my security. I'm sure you can imagine how it is," he said somberly, and she nodded. "I don't want to cause a fuss." He forced a slight smile, and the lady handed him visitor passes. He and Rachel went up to the second floor and down to the ICU.

He headed down the hallway. Two children, about eight and ten, stood outside the room, and then a pair of littler ones stopped in the doorway.

"Bye, Grandpa Adam," one of the little ones said. The others crowded into the doorway, waving and saying goodbye. Then a figure from Lucas's past stepped out of the room.

Lucas knew him instantly. Hell, he'd know Matthew Wilson anywhere, even after all these years. He took the younger ones by the hand, and the entire little group turned Lucas's way.

Lucas couldn't breathe for a second, and he wasn't even sure Matthew noticed him. When Matthew paused and lifted the smallest little boy into his arms, Lucas said gently, "Matthew."

Matthew turned, eyes widening, and then his lips curled into a smile. "Lucas." He turned back toward Lucas's father's room. "I got special permission to bring the kids up to say goodbye." His smile faded. "This is Will, Gregory, Brianna, and Carl." He indicated each from oldest to youngest and smiled at the boy in his arms. "They're my sister Eden's children."

"Grandpa Adam is dying," Carl said before burying his face in Matthew's shirt. "Like Mommy and Daddy."

Well, that answered half the questions running through Lucas's head.

"I need to get them home," Matthew said, and their little group continued down the hall. Lucas couldn't help turning to watch Matthew go, and noticed that he looked over his shoulder before reaching the bend in the hall.

"Old friend of yours?" Rachel asked.

Lucas nodded. "The one I let get away." And the man he had thought about almost every day since he left town. He went to the room and stepped inside.

His father lay on the hospital bed, eyes closed. Lucas was tempted to leave, but then his father's eyes slid open, so Lucas came forward. "Aunt Rose said you were asking for me."

His father blinked and opened his mouth, but no words came out. He raised his hand, and Lucas took it. For so many years he had hated this man. Every time he needed to bring up a well of emotion or strong, deep hatred in a movie, he thought of him, and every director and critic remarked on the power of his performances. But now, standing here next to him, none of that mattered. His father had always seemed so big, and now there was very little left of him.

"I never understood," he whispered as he squeezed Lucas's hand.

"What, Dad?" he asked softly.

"I never understood, but I do now." He squeezed Lucas's hand a final time, and then his fingers went lax.

The beeping of the monitor stopped, and Lucas turned away. At least he had made it in time.

CHAPTER 2

MATTHEW GOT the kids into the van, and Will helped make sure the younger ones were buckled in. He hurried around the driver's side as the rain picked up. The door squeaked as he closed it. Matthew sighed and pulled out the keys to start the engine. It clicked, but nothing more. "Danged thing," he muttered as he tried again. Nothing. The lights were on, but the starter must have failed. "All of you stay here."

He popped the hood, and just his luck, the skies opened up as he lifted it to try to access the starter. A lot of the time, if he tapped it, the thing would turn over. He managed to reach it and then went back into the car, sloshing in his shoes as he tried the ignition again. No luck.

"Uncle Daddy, can we go home now?" Brianna asked.

"I'm trying, sweethearts." He closed his eyes and prayed to the god of cars to let this bucket of bolts start and get them all home. After that, the damned thing could die forever. "Give me a minute."

After getting out, he lifted the hood once more and tried to do whatever he could.

"Matthew."

He turned, the rain running down his face, soaking him to the skin. The window of a huge SUV rolled down, and Lucas Reardon looked at him. A face he had seen in his mind for years and one he'd watched in the theaters and on the small screen, never missing a movie, TV appearance, or Netflix series. "It's dead and I can't start it."

"Are the kids inside?"

He nodded, feeling more miserable by the second.

"Rachel, pull around." The window rolled up and the SUV pulled away, made a circuit of the lot, and came up on the sliding door side of the van. "Get the kids in here, and we'll get you all home."

Matthew was out of options. He pulled open the sliding door. "Okay, guys. Mr. Lucas is going to give us a ride home. Get your things and be careful." He lifted Carl into his arms, and as soon as the driver stepped out with an umbrella, he transferred Carl to the SUV, the other three hurrying over. Matthew checked for bags and things left behind, then unhooked Carl's car seat and the boosters for the others. The driver got them inside while he locked the van and got into the Navigator himself.

Will had the boosters for the middle two installed way in the back, and the driver had the car seat secured. Soon all the kids were seated, and Matthew climbed in back in the middle and closed the door. "Thank you." He was at his wits' end.

"You're Lucas Reardon, the movie star," Will said, his voice filled with awe. "You know Uncle Daddy?"

"I'm hungry," Carl said. "And I gotta go potty."

All Matthew could do was hang his head. There were times when he wondered why Eden and Jack had left the care of their children to him. Fuck both of them and that drunk driver who had sent their car off a bridge.

"Okay. What do you like to eat?"

"Nuggets."

"Chicken."

"Hamburgers." Each of the youngest three had an opinion. Matthew noticed that Will said nothing.

"Okay. Rachel, let's find a restaurant. I know there are some downtown. We can get the kids fed and use the bathroom." The car started forward, and Matthew pulled out his soaked wallet, wondering what he was going to get the kids on the twenty dollars that was all he had in the world right now.

"Do you really know Uncle Daddy?" Will asked Lucas.

"Yes. He and your mom and I went to high school together." Lucas turned with that smile Matthew had seen so many times in person and on the screen. "Matthew and I were really good friends." He caught Matthew's gaze for just a second, and Matthew felt a wave of heat run through him. It lasted only a few seconds, and then the fact that he was wet to the bone chilled away everything. "It's been a long time since we saw each other, but I like to think that he and I will always be friends."

Matthew nodded. There was no way he was going to hate Lucas. He couldn't blame him for getting out of the area when he had the chance. Most of the people he'd known in high school had wanted to leave, and many had gone away to college and never returned for more than a few days. Still, he and Lucas had had something special—at least he thought they had. But the lure of the chance to act had been too good for Lucas to pass up. Matthew had hoped to be able to join him, but family needs and life in general had intervened, and Matthew ended up going nowhere.

Rachel parked in front of the restaurant, and the kids got excited as they peered out the windows. The rain had let up again, and Rachel got out of the car and, with Will's help, got the kids inside. "I have a bag in back." Lucas used the break in the rain to get out some clothes. He passed a pair of light sweatpants and a shirt over the back of the seat. "I don't have any shoes that will fit you."

"I know. They'd fall off. You have huge feet."

Lucas's head popped up over the seat, that grin in place, and for a second they were high school seniors again. "And you know what they say about men with big feet… 'cause it's true and you know it." He winked, and Matthew laughed, deep and loud. He almost ended up crying, it felt so good just to let go, even for a few seconds. "It wasn't that funny… or even original."

Everything had been so tough lately. "I guess it's been long enough that you seem funny, or maybe it's living with four kids, and adult conversation is like water in the desert." He took the clothes and grabbed the to-go bag he always had with him. With four kids, he was never without the basics, like granola bars, socks, underwear, small bottles of water, and Tylenol.

Lucas closed the back, and they went inside. Rachel and Will had all the kids at a table, and Lucas joined them while Matthew went in search of a bathroom, hoping he didn't leave puddles with each step.

"UNCLE DADDY," Brianna called when he came back, his wet things in a plastic bag, "I can see your nipples." She giggled, and Matthew laughed as he took the empty chair across from Lucas, between her and Carl. He felt more human in dry clothes and was grateful his shoes somehow hadn't been soaked through, but the shirt he was wearing was at least a size too small, and it stretched over him like a second skin. When the kids said something uncomfortable, he had learned to just ignore it and hope that the subject would end.

"Did you really fly when you played Superboy?" Will asked.

Lucas shook his head. "It's all movie magic. They put me in this harness and then they fly me in front of a special screen. After that, they take out what they don't want and put in everything else with the computer, so in the end it looks like I'm flying, but the whole time I was no more than two feet off the ground."

"Did you really kiss Paula Greer? I like her," Brianna said.

Lucas nodded. "But it was a movie kiss, not a real one. Paula is very nice." He spent a good ten minutes patiently answering all the kids' questions. When the server came to the table, she did a double take and shook her head. There was no way Matthew was going to make the kids sit here and not eat, so he just hoped he had room on one of his credit cards. He helped each of them order and then got something for himself.

"Sir?" she asked Lucas, who ordered a salad. Rachel placed her order as well and then got up and wandered toward the back of the restaurant.

"Where is she going?" Matthew asked quietly, just before Carl took Brianna's fork and she snatched it back, which ended in shouting and tears. "That's enough, both of you," Matthew said sharply. "You have your own fork," he said and handed it to him before soothing Brianna with a light touch.

"Rachel is checking out the room, making sure she knows all the exits and things. It's what she does." Lucas seemed relaxed.

"But…."

Lucas shrugged. "Last year I had a stalker who decided that watching and sending messages wasn't enough. Rachel helped me out and was able to catch the guy. She's very good at what she does." Rachel checked out front and then returned to the table.

Matthew had always wondered what it would be like to see Lucas again and if he'd even remember him. But now that he was sitting right across from him, he didn't know what to talk about. The two of them had been in each other's back pockets when they'd been in school and that year of college together. Matthew knew everything about Lucas back then. They hadn't had any secrets and had shared everything: their hopes, dreams, hearts… everything. But now Lucas was a huge movie star, and Matthew was still in the same town. Granted, he had the kids, and he wouldn't trade the four of them for anything in the world.

Rachel sat back down and then started talking to Brianna. Matthew smiled as his little girl, who was normally rather quiet, opened up to Rachel. She and Will even traded places so she could sit across from Rachel.

"What else have you been doing besides raising the kids?" Lucas asked. "They must keep you busy."

"I'm an electrician. I finished my stint as a journeyman two years ago, just before the accident, and I maintain all the equipment at the vegetable processing plant." It was a good job, and he was grateful to have it. The pay wasn't great, but he had benefits that covered him and the kids.

Lucas looked down the table, half smiling, and then leaned closer. "How did you know my father...? I mean...?"

Matthew shrugged. "I hadn't seen him for years after you left, but then he started volunteering for youth baseball, and Will is an amazing player. And after Eden passed, he was there for us. The kids all call him Grandpa Adam." He felt himself choke up. Matthew was now one step closer to loneliness. Adam had been there when the kids needed him. He'd helped Will through his grieving and given him something to look forward to. "Adam connected with the kids. He was their cheerleader, never missed a game or a school concert." Hell, he was a friend, and now he was gone. Matthew had known that Adam had little time left, and had done his best to try to prepare the kids.

Lucas seemed a little lost as well. "I'm glad he was there for you." His lips grew tight, and Matthew had a pretty good idea what Lucas was thinking. It was a shame that Adam hadn't been there for Lucas in the way he had for Matthew and his family. Maybe Adam felt that the kids were a way to make up for what he hadn't done with Lucas. They would never know now.

"I'm happy you're here. It—" Matthew paused as squeals went up from another table. Three girls and a teenage boy hurried over.

"Oh my God, you're—"

"Lucas Reardon," another girl finished, bouncing up and down.

"I can't believe it's you. Can I have your autograph?" All three of the girls bounced while the boy looked on in awe.

Lucas smiled and signed something for each of them while Rachel tensed next to him.

Once the kids returned to their table, talking excitedly, Rachel headed back through the restaurant, and after a few minutes, she returned and sat down, looking for all the world like she was ready to step into action at any moment.

"Does that happen a lot?" Will asked.

Lucas shrugged. "Sometimes. It's okay, though." He smiled, but Matthew knew it was one of tension. He remembered that same smile and bravado as they went into a big test.

"Can I get your autograph too?" Will asked.

"Of course you can. But how about after lunch? We can get a picture with all of us. Okay?" Lucas asked before turning back to Matthew. "I really think I'd like one of those." The longing and loneliness in Lucas's voice rang through, if even only to Matthew.

"That would be nice."

Rachel cleared her throat. "The restaurant has agreed not to admit anyone else until we leave," she told Lucas.

"Do you do that a lot?" Matthew asked.

Lucas sighed. "I haven't been able to go out to dinner without a huge production in years. The last time I went to the movies, I had to go in costume so no one would recognize me. When I'm in LA, I have a security staff that stays with me, and every time I leave the house, someone is always trying to take my picture. The last time I needed to buy clothes, the store was mobbed, and I had to be ushered back to the car."

Their food arrived, and a few people stopped by the table on their way out. Lucas greeted each one, shook hands, and gave them a smile before returning to his lunch. But after each time, that light in his eyes dimmed a little and he became more drawn. It had to be exhausting.

Lucas took care of the bill, and all four kids thanked him.

"Let's use the bathroom before we go home." They traipsed back toward the restrooms. "Thank you for lunch and the ride. And please let me know when the service will be. They'll all want to be there."

"Of course." Lucas stood, and before Matthew could react, one of the most famous people in the country hugged him tightly. "Maybe we can see each other again before I go back."

"I'd like that," Matthew said. Lucas released him, and Matthew made sure he had everything as the kids returned. Then they all headed for the door together.

THE RAIN had stopped, but water still puddled on the roads as they drove east out of Ludington, toward Scottville. Matthew gave Rachel the address, and she got them home quickly. Lucas was quiet for much of the drive, not that Matthew could blame him.

"This is your sister's house," Lucas said when they pulled into the drive.

"They left it to me for the kids," Matthew told him. He had intended to sell it, but then he'd needed a place for all five of them to live, so he kept it and they stayed. "Come on, guys. I have to call and have the van towed." He got them all out just as the rain began again. The kids said goodbye to Lucas and Rachel before Will unlocked the house and let them inside.

The passenger-side window slid down, and Matthew went up to it. Lucas smiled at him, and just before he left, Matthew gave him a business card with his number on it.

"Thank you," Lucas said.

"I'll get your clothes back to you." He stepped back as the car started forward. For the second time, Matthew watched as Lucas slipped away, wishing he knew the words to stop him.

"Uncle Daddy, you're getting wet," Brianna called.

Matthew went inside, closing the door behind him. He looked around the living room—toys piled in the corner, his mother's old furniture still in the same place, only now covered with throws and blankets.

Carl tugged at his sleeve, and Matthew sat down while his youngest curled against him. "I'm going to miss Grandpa," he said softly.

"I know. We all are."

"Are you going to die too?" Carl asked while Brianna and the others all sat next to him.

"Nope. I'm going to stay here with you forever." He hugged each of them and kissed their foreheads. Well, everyone's but Will, who was too old for that sort of thing. "Why don't you all get your chores done, okay?"

The rain picked up again, coming down hard, echoing Matthew's feelings. But there was no time for him to be sad. The kids needed him, and there were things to be done. So all he could do was get to it. Even if when he closed his eyes, all he saw was a face that had always seemed so close. But once again, Lucas was out of his reach and would stay that way.

CHAPTER 3

"YOU NEED to be at your aunt's in half an hour," Rachel said as she popped her head into the bedroom of their suite.

Lucas groaned. "Okay. I'm getting up." He checked the time, did a quick calculation, and groaned again. He was used to getting up at five in the morning to be on set, but after all that travel, he was still worn out. It didn't help that the clock might read eight, but he hadn't gotten to sleep until well after two. "What does one wear to a funeral-planning session?" he asked.

"Something that doesn't make one look like an asshole," Rachel retorted, and Lucas glared at her. "Casual pants and a light shirt. The sun is out, and it's going to be hot and humid today. I'll have coffee and something light ready for you." She closed the door, and Lucas got up, stretched, and took a quick shower. He dressed in light tan pants and a plum shirt before leaving his room. Rachel had coffee, fruit, and an english muffin on the table for him. Lucas sat and ate mechanically, his mind not really processing things yet.

"There are some messages from Karen. I answered them already. But she says you need to call your agent today, and she sends you a hug and all the feel-better vibes she can muster. Her exact words." Rachel smiled.

"Karen is special." He finished the fruit and half the muffin before downing his coffee. He had had enough to eat, so he threw the rest away. "Let's go."

Lucas didn't quite know what to feel as he rode. His father was gone. Thankfully, they had made some sort of peace before he passed, but now Lucas wished they might have had more time.

"Regrets suck," Rachel said out of the blue. "Don't have any."

"Do you read minds too?" Lucas asked.

Rachel scoffed. "Your father died, and you hadn't talked to him for a long time. Regret sort of comes with the territory." She pulled to a stop at a light. "But it's useless, and it takes two to tango. Your father could have contacted you. He didn't, so stop putting this on yourself. You had a moment with your father, which is more than most others get. Carry that with you instead of the rest."

Lucas wanted to snap at her, at someone, but hell, she was right. Things were what they were, and he did get some closure. He had been there with his dad when he died, and there was nothing more he could have done. "Are you usually this talkative with your clients?"

"No. And if you want me to shut up, I will." She started forward. "But I know what it feels like to lose a parent and not be there. My mother passed two years ago when I was with Carson Meyers in Bangkok. There was no way I could get home in time." Her voice stayed steady, but Lucas heard the pain. "You have to look for the good things and let go of the rest or it will eat you alive."

He turned to Rachel. "Thanks." Most people wouldn't have bothered.

They turned into the funeral home parking lot. Aunt Rose was outside waiting. "I'm going to wait out here and watch things," Rachel said.

Lucas got out of the car and hugged his aunt. "Is it just us?"

Aunt Rose hugged him back before shaking her head. Then she led him inside to a room with sofas and comfortable chairs. Matthew and the kids sat together. Will got up and came right over to shake Lucas's his hand. Gregory sat next to Matthew, the shy boy looking like he wanted to disappear. Brianna came over to him, and when he knelt down, she hugged him.

"I'm sorry about your daddy," she said with tears running down her cheeks. He hugged her again, and she went right into his arms. Lucas sat down, and she climbed into his lap. Carl had apparently taken possession of Matthew's.

"And I'm sorry about your Grandpa Adam," he said, his throat aching. He looked over her to Matthew and then to his aunt.

"Matthew called last night and told me that the kids wanted to be part of the service." She cleared her throat. "They were a big part of his life the past few years."

"I see." Not that he had any objection, or even a right to make one.

The funeral director came in and sat down quietly. He spoke softly and explained what they would be doing. Everything had already been picked out and paid for. "It's just the order of service we need to discuss."

"The kids wanted to be part of it. Will asked if he could do one of the readings. He's very good. The others will go up with him." Matthew wiped his eyes, and Brianna pressed closer to Lucas. He closed his arms around her, not sure if he was comforting her or if just having her in his arms was keeping him grounded.

"What about you? As his son?" The funeral director turned to Lucas, who shook his head.

"This isn't about me. If I say something or get up front, it will be a distraction. Let Will and others take the lead on this." He sat back as Aunt Rose took over. She and Matthew figured out hymns and other things. Lucas largely sat still, listening, and was grateful when it was over. The funeral home would arrange for an announcement in the paper, and the memorial service would be in a few days. Dad had opted for cremation, so there wouldn't be a casket or visitation.

Once they were done, Matthew and the kids followed them out. Lucas had wondered about the good of bringing them to something like this, but Will and Gregory seemed to have ideas about how they wanted to say goodbye to Grandpa Adam, and as they left, they seemed to feel better, and so did Lucas.

Rachel stood near the car, waiting for him. "Do you need a ride home?" Lucas asked Matthew.

"Could you do that?" Aunt Rose asked.

"Of course. What about the van?"

"They said they'll be able to fix it today," Matthew answered. "Thank goodness." Now that they were outside with the sun shining, the funeral gloom seemed to have lifted, at least for now. They went through the process of getting the seats set back up in the SUV, and then everyone piled inside.

"What do you all have to do today?" Lucas asked and received silence in return.

"Maybe grocery shopping," Matthew finally said to a chorus of groans.

"Can we go to the park?" Gregory asked quietly.

"Swimming?" Brianna chimed in.

"Ice cream," Carl chirped.

Lucas turned around in his seat. "We could go out to the state park if you like. We don't have their suits with us, but the kids can run around."

"Are you sure that's a good idea?" Rachel asked. "It's a very open space."

"It should be fine. There aren't going to be a bunch of reporters lined up out there waiting to surround me."

Rachel shook her head. "True, but it has been reported in the press that your father passed away and that you are in town for the funeral. People will be looking for you."

"Not out at the park, with everyone having a good time enjoying their vacation or their time off. They aren't going to be looking for me. I think it will be fine." And he was looking for some fresh air. Lucas had spent weeks in sound stages, on planes, and in that damned trailer. He needed a chance to be outside. Lucas gave Rachel directions, and they were off toward the state park.

At the entrance, Lucas paid the fee, and then Rachel drove all the way through to the parking lot at Hamlin Lake. "Do you want to walk over the dam?" Lucas asked, and the kids got all excited. "Rachel?"

"I'll be around," she answered.

"Matthew, is that okay?" he asked.

"Sure. Let's go."

They all headed off, the kids talking a mile a minute. Will and Gregory held hands with the others as they walked down the path, the roar of the water growing louder.

"You didn't have to do this," Matthew said. "We could have just gone home."

Carl and Brianna hurried back. "What is it?"

"Loud," Carl said, and Matthew picked him up. Lucas offered Brianna his hand, and she took it.

The older two watched the water cascade over the dam as Lucas and Matthew approached. "I can take her if you want," Matthew offered.

"She's good," Lucas said with a smile as they started over the top of the dam. Brianna vibrated with excitement as they made their way over to the other side. Then she hurried off toward her brothers. Matthew set Carl down, and he raced over the sand after her. "We used to come here."

"Yeah. Remember the time they brought our class on that school trip and we snuck off?" Matthew asked.

Lucas snickered. "How could I forget it? We climbed that dune, and when the teachers weren't looking, we disappeared into the woods. It was supposed to be an earth science class, but for you and me it was very much about biology." He turned to Matthew, whose eyes held a faraway look.

"Things were so simple back then." Their gazes trailed upward. "Sometimes I wish they were now as well." Matthew closed his eyes, face still turned toward the sky. Lucas watched him, his heart already warming. "You know, I hated you for a while."

"Uncle Daddy, do we have any toys?" Carl asked, tugging on Matthew's pant leg. Then he looked over at a small pavilion with things for sale.

"I tried to stop him," Will said. "Come on, Carl. We can make things with our hands."

Lucas pulled out his wallet and handed Will a couple of twenties. "Get whatever you guys want, okay? Something for each of you. Just be careful the money doesn't blow away."

Will put the bills in his pocket, and all four kids hurried over to the booth, with Carl calling for them to wait up.

"You didn't have to do that," Matthew said. "They would have been fine."

"I know." He sat on one of the concrete embankments. "But you remember what it was like growing up here. We didn't have anything. Dad worked his piece of land and he provided for us as best he could, but there were no luxuries. Certainly not money for pails and sand toys, other than the ones Mom found at garage sales."

Carl grinned as he walked back toward them carrying a net bag full of toys. "Look what I got." He held it up and plopped down in the sand a few feet away. Lucas helped him open the bag, and the others joined him in the sand.

Will handed Lucas back a twenty. "Thank you," he said shyly and then smiled.

"You're welcome."

"You all need to play nicely," Matthew said as the younger three settled in to play. Will wandered down the beach and sat on the concrete wall a little ways away, looking out over the water.

"You were saying?" Lucas said. "That you hated me...." God, he hoped there was more to be said than that.

"I did. You left, and I hated you for it just because I was stuck here and always would be. Then I started seeing you in movies. I was so jealous, and yet I went to every single one. I have them at home too. I used to save them at the parts you were in so I could see your face."

Lucas smiled and pulled out his wallet. He tugged out a picture from one of the pockets. "Remember this?" It was of the two of them. Lucas's mom had taken it. They stood on one of the bridges, with the water in the background. "It's been with me always."

Matthew's lips drew straight, and his eyes narrowed in a sort of "don't fuck with me" gaze. "I saw all the stories about the guys you dated."

Lucas laughed. "I went to awards shows and concerts with them; we didn't date." He leaned closer and lowered his voice. "We may have fucked once or twice, but I never dated anyone."

Matthew swallowed. "No one?"

Lucas shook his head.

"Why?"

Lucas shrugged.

"Why, Lucas?" he asked. "You had plenty of people who wanted you. The tabloids were full of rumors. I read tons of online articles about you and who you were interested in."

"Yeah. Maybe. But that stuff is mostly lies and speculation. I never went out with anyone more than three times, and I never dated anyone. I took people to awards dinners, charity events, things like that, but none of them ever saw the inside of my house. Because like I said, I don't date."

"But you could have," Matthew pressed.

Lucas found himself getting annoyed. He wished Matthew would back off, but then, Matthew had always been tenacious when he wanted something.

"There had to be a lot of people you worked with or ones who liked you."

"Can we just drop it?" Lucas asked. "I was busy, and everyone thinks making movies is easy. It isn't. I spend a lot of time away from home and a lot of weeks where I stay in my trailer because it's easier than going home at all. There isn't time for a relationship." He shrugged and hoped Matthew bought his explanation. Everything he said was true, but he couldn't tell Matthew the real reason. It wouldn't be fair to either of them. As much as Lucas wished he could simply hold Matthew in his arms, he couldn't. Matthew had a life here, one that involved four kids, and it was only a matter of time before Lucas had to return to Hollywood. The clock was ticking. This trip home was only a short interlude.

He slipped off the wall they had been sitting on and went to where the kids were digging a hole. "What are you making?" he asked.

"Big castle," Carl answered, pointing to a pile of sand. He dumped his bucketful on the top before industriously working to fill it again. "You help?" He handed Lucas the pail. He filled it and dumped more sand onto Carl's pile.

His phone rang, and Lucas considered ignoring it, but very few people had this number. He pulled it out of his pocket. "What is it, Rachel?"

"There are pictures of you playing in the sand with Carl all over Instagram. Like, they're blowing up."

"Okay. It happens." Lucas set down the pail and stood. Half a dozen people had their phones out, all pointed in his direction. "Yeah, I can see I'm the center of attention."

"I'm on my way," she said.

"No, it's fine. If we overreact, then it will be even worse. Just come and join us and make sure nothing else happens." He hung up and went back to playing in the sand.

"What is all that about?" Matthew asked, and Lucas explained. "I take it that happens a lot."

Lucas nodded. "Rachel is on her way, and she'll make sure everyone leaves us alone." He settled back on his knees. "The kids are having fun, and I don't want to stop them."

"Uncle Daddy, I need to go potty," Carl said.

"Can you watch the other three? I'll be right back." Matthew took Carl by the hand and led him down the path along the river toward the bathrooms. Lucas played with the others, helping them with their castles. Rachel strode across the sand, kicking up clouds as she went. Then she took up a position behind where Lucas and the kids were playing. He stifled a snicker as she stared down anyone who so much as held their phone up.

"Dang," Lucas told her. "Don't look at the water or it will freeze."

Brianna jumped up. "I wanna see that." She hurried toward the lake, and Lucas snatched her up and flew her back to the others.

"Sorry. It was just an expression," Lucas told her. "Rachel can't really freeze the water." Though if it were possible, she'd figure out a way to do it.

"Awww," Brianna said. She was adorable. All the kids were cool.

Matthew returned with Carl, and the kids settled down to play again. Lucas sat next to Matthew, enjoying the sun and a few hours without pressure.

"We should go," Rachel said after about half an hour alternating between watching the people nearby and checking her phone. "People are putting out where to find you, and there's someone making threats."

Matthew got right into action. "Okay, guys, let's get ready to go. Pick up your toys and put them back in the bag."

Rachel watched as Lucas and Matthew helped the kids. Then Matthew lifted Carl and took Gregory's hand. Rachel stayed with Will, and Lucas held Brianna's hand as a large group of people started approaching. They crossed the dam, and Rachel passed Will to him. "You all go right to the car." She handed Lucas the keys. "I'm going to stop them on the dam. Then I'll join you." She stayed at the entrance, blocking anyone from returning until they were well ahead.

"That was fun," Carl said with a grin.

"Were those bad people?" Brianna asked.

Lucas shook his head. "Not necessarily. But there were a lot of them, and sometimes people want to be close to someone famous, so it was safer if we left."

"It's a 'just in case' thing," Will told her, and she seemed to accept it. Clearly, "just in case" things were something these kids had dealt with before.

Rachel strode over and met them at the SUV. They got in with a minimum of fuss, and Rachel got them out of the parking lot before anyone could follow too closely.

"Where to?" Rachel asked.

Lucas turned. "Do you and the kids have any place you need to be?" Matthew shook his head. "Do you all have bathing suits?" Matthew smiled and nodded. "Then let's go get them. The hotel has a water park of sorts, and we might as well put it to use." He loved the look of surprise in Matthew's eyes.

"Good idea," Rachel told him, as serious as a heart attack. Lucas turned toward her as she drove and tried to read her expression, which was all business. "One of the pictures was originally posted by Ruetoyou."

Lucas swallowed hard. "You mean the stalker from last year? I thought he was gone." His chest tightened.

"Apparently he went underground but has resurfaced, and he was in the crowd of people at the park." She lowered her voice. "The asshole followed you home."

Lucas gasped and turned toward the back seat, his breath coming quickly.

"Remember, the guy never did anything other than try to get close to you all the time. He has an obsession with you and wants to get your attention. Just like before, though, he isn't necessarily dangerous." She stayed calm, and that sank into Lucas. "I have your back."

Lucas nodded, but all he could think about was Matthew and the kids. Was he putting them in danger?

"Stop catastrophizing." She smiled at him. "This is part of what you have me here for."

"But we don't know what he looks like." The guy was like a ghost, and that's what scared him most of all.

CHAPTER 4

RACHEL SHRUGGED. "Maybe not completely. We never got pictures of him."

"But I might have," Matthew said. The kids hadn't been paying attention to the conversation between Lucas and Rachel, but he had. "I took a ton of pictures of the scenery, as well as the kids playing." He'd also taken a lot of pictures of Lucas, because what could be more endearing than Lucas being a kid with his kids? "If this guy was there, then I might have gotten a picture of him. And chances are you've seen this guy and didn't know it, so maybe you'll recognize him."

Lucas flashed him a smile Matthew hadn't seen in years. "You're the best." He reached behind the seats and patted Matthew's leg, a gesture that brought memories flooding back.

"This guy is a master at keeping out of sight, and yet he keeps being able to get near me. I came close to catching him a year ago, and we thought we had scared him off. The incidents stopped suddenly, and it's been a long time. But he's back now," Lucas said, his voice filled with worry.

"Why did he stop?" Matthew asked, leaning forward to talk quietly. It seemed like the obvious question to him. The kids seemed to be paying attention now, though, so Matthew sat back again. This conversation could wait until later.

Rachel took them home, and it took a while to find all the bathing suits and get each of the kids into theirs, pack bags of dry clothes, then pack a small cooler of juice boxes and snacks and make sure everyone had gone potty. Matthew was so wrapped up in getting the kids ready that he nearly forgot his own bathing suit, but he stuffed it and a towel in with the things for the kids before all of them traipsed out of the small ranch-style home that his sister and brother-in-law had left to him.

"Did you bring my floaties?" Brianna asked.

"And mine?" Carl questioned once Matthew got everything inside the SUV and sat down.

"I swear I brought half the house," Matthew said, hoping Lucas didn't decide that they just weren't worth it. He put on his seat belt and they rode back toward town, where they pulled into the parking lot of the large chain hotel. It had once been a Holiday Inn, then a Ramada, and now it had yet another name on the sign, but it was the best this area had to offer, in terms of amenities.

Rachel parked, and Lucas strode through the lobby like he owned the place, while Matthew and the kids trailed behind him like a line of ducks. Matthew kept an eye on the kids and their surroundings while they made their way to Lucas's huge suite. "You can all get ready in here, and I'll be out in a few minutes. Then we'll go down to the pool." He grinned. Brianna and Carl bounced, they were so excited.

"Okay," Matthew said, settling the three youngest on the sofa while Will sat in a chair. "You all need to be good. No running around the pool, and no jumping in when I'm not around." He turned to Gregory, who was fearless when it came to water. It scared Matthew to death sometimes. "No going in the big pool without me, okay?" Gregory groaned, but Matthew stayed firm until he agreed. "I'm going to get into my bathing suit." He gave them all a firm glare before going into the bathroom to change.

Matthew was pleased and half shocked that all four kids were still in their places and the room hadn't been torn to shreds while he'd been in the bathroom. There had been times when he left them in front of the TV only to return after relieving himself to find two crying kids pointing fingers at each other with something broken on the floor and Carl with a cut on his finger from broken glass.

"Can we go now?" Gregory asked.

"Shhh," Will said. "We need to be good, and we need to wait for Lucas and Miss Rachel." Sometimes Will was so grown up it worried Matthew. He was eleven and often acted much older. He worried that Will's childhood was being taken away from him. Matthew sat as well, waiting for Lucas, wondering how much longer he could keep the energy of four excited kids from exploding.

"Are you ready?" Lucas asked as he came out of the other room in board shorts and a T-shirt.

Carl hurried over to him. "We were good and waited and everything," he blurted.

Lucas smiled and took his hand. "Then let's go down to the pool." Matthew got the bags, and they all followed Lucas like he was the Pied Piper.

Rachel locked the room and followed them down the hall. She didn't say anything, and as soon as they entered the pool area, she scoped out a place where she could watch everything, then secured the area before taking a seat at one of the tables.

"Why here?" Matthew asked her.

"It has good sight lines, and it's close to the regular and kiddie pools." She was all business and seemed wound as tight as a drum. Matthew nodded and went over the rules with the kids, making them say them back.

"We know. We can't go in the big pool without you, and we have to have our swimmies on," Brianna told him like it was a real chore. She took Carl by the hand, and they stepped into the kiddie pool. Matthew had floaty toys for them. Will and Gregory were at that age where they could both swim, but he wasn't ready to leave them alone in the pool.

"Play in the water here, and I'll go in the other pool with you both in a little while," Matthew promised.

"Okay," Will agreed and sat on the edge of the kiddie pool with his feet in the water. Gregory played with his brother and sister while Matthew sat down.

Lucas had been on the other side of the room talking on the phone. He joined him at the table and sat as well. His shirt was drawn tight around his arms and chest, giving Matthew a glimpse of the toned body underneath. He had seen Lucas shirtless in various movies, but having him so close in person sent his heart racing.

"Is everything okay?" Matthew asked.

"Yes. I had to check in with my agent. Everything is fine." Lucas was lying, judging by the small lines around his eyes. Matthew leaned forward, meeting Lucas's gaze until he looked away. "It's no big deal. The movie I was set to start next had to be postponed a week. That's going to throw off my schedule for months. My agent is trying to get everything worked out." He sat back, and Matthew turned to Rachel, who simply shrugged like that was how things were.

"Does that happen a lot?" Matthew asked.

"More than it should. I just need to get my head around it." He sat back, rippling with tension Matthew was pretty sure had little to do with a schedule change.

Rather than press it, Matthew handed Rachel his phone and let her go through the pictures he'd taken at the park. "Text yourself any you want," he told her, and she got to work. Matthew watched the kids play in the otherwise empty space. "Where is everyone else?"

"I arranged for two hours to ourselves. Unfortunately, it seems to be the only way I can get some peace." Lucas sighed as Rachel continued looking through the pictures. Matthew pulled off his shirt and stood.

"Come on, munchkins." He lifted Carl into his arms and took Brianna by the hand. "Let's go in the other pool. All of you need to stay in the shallow end."

"Can we go down the slide?" Will asked, and Matthew agreed. Brianna hurried ahead and got right in the water. She was totally fearless. Carl put his arms around Matthew's neck, and they walked in together. He wasn't as comfortable and held on, which was fine.

Lucas approached the water and tested it with his foot. Then he pulled off his shirt, and Matthew swallowed hard as all that smooth skin over taut muscle came into view. Damn, he was more stunning in person, and Matthew forgot where he was for a few seconds. "Uncle Daddy," Carl prompted, and Matthew continued into the water, grateful for the coolness to quench the heat that threatened to build.

Lucas glided into the water, then dove under the surface, moving easily through the water. Will came down the slide. He laughed as he came up for air before swimming toward Lucas. Gregory went after him, heading right for the side of the pool.

"Uncle Daddy, watch me," Brianna called, and she jumped in the water.

"That's good, honey. Just be careful, okay?" She nodded and was already climbing out of the pool, getting ready to jump again. Matthew watched, and then Carl let go. He began doing his own version of swimming.

"They're pretty amazing," Lucas said as he stood next to him. The water was slightly cool, but in an instant, Matthew felt warm and did his best to watch the kids rather than let his attention wander to Lucas, because damn… he wanted to lick—or *look*, yeah, that was the right word, especially with the kids all around—the man over from top to bottom.

"They are," Matthew managed to say, his voice rough because Lucas was right next to him. If Matthew reached out, he could touch the man he wished he hadn't let get away.

"Why do some of them call you Uncle Daddy?" Lucas asked.

Brianna raced up to the edge of the pool, tears running down her cheeks. "I falled," she reported and showed Matthew her knee. There was a little red spot, and he kissed his fingers and placed them over the spot.

"Is that better?" he asked, and she nodded. Matthew hugged her, and then she was off again. "The older ones remember their mom and dad pretty well. I keep pictures in the house so they don't forget them." He leaned against the side of the pool so he could see all the kids, and Lucas stood next to him, heat washing off his radiant skin. For a second, Matthew forgot what he'd been talking about. "Brianna started calling me Daddy one day, and it really upset Will." He turned to face Lucas. "And I understand that. Those kids already had a dad and a mom who they lost. So I asked Will what he thought the kids should call me, and he came up with Uncle Daddy. When he told the younger two, it stuck."

Lucas shook his head. "You're pretty amazing, you know that? Not many people would think to ask him. They'd just do what they wanted."

"I know. But he was hurting—we all were. I was trying to figure out how I was going to see four kids through college and make sure I didn't completely mess them up." He lowered his gaze. "And I can tell you, this is the hardest job I have ever had… and the best one." Matthew followed all of the kids, making sure they were safe. Brianna and Carl played in the kiddie pool while the older two swam in the shallow end.

"I can only imagine," Lucas said. "I dated someone against my better judgment a few years ago. He was an actor in one of the films I made. He had a boy who was about Brianna's age, and he brought him to the set when he wasn't in school. Nice kid, but hugely spoiled."

"I see."

"Nathan and I weren't going to work out. I can see that now. He was most likely using me to try to get ahead, and Jason was out of control. He had issues with his father seeing anyone. I think when Nathan and his mother separated, he got very attached to his father." Lucas bumped Matthew's shoulder. "I also think the kid played the parents against each other so he could get everything he wanted. It was a pretty difficult situation, and I have to say, I'm glad I broke it off. It wasn't going to be healthy."

"Well, these kids aren't spoiled, and I don't think they ever will be. I don't have enough resources to spoil them. I do make sure they get as much attention as I can give them." He waved when Gregory called to him to watch.

"That's obvious." He shifted closer, and Matthew tensed as excitement grew. He was glad his waist was below the water. "But what's also evident is that they're happy, and that's what really matters. Nathan's son was never happy. He always wanted something, and then as soon as he got it, he was on to the next thing. There was nothing stable in his life. Nathan moved from place to place and set to set, and Jason had no stability."

Rachel came over and squatted down near the water.

"Miss Rachel, come play with us," Gregory called.

"Maybe later, okay?" she said with a smile before turning to Lucas. "I think I have some things you need to look at."

"Okay." Lucas climbed out of the pool, his suit tightening around his legs and ass. Damn, the man was stunning from every angle. Matthew looked, probably for longer than he should have, before diving under the water to try to clear his mind. Then he swam over to the kids, and Will challenged him to a race. Gregory started them, while the two youngest cheered them on. Matthew won because he didn't believe in letting people win, but Will was right behind him.

"Dang," Will said when he reached the other side.

"Hey," Matthew told him. "You're getting good, and someday pretty soon, you will be faster than me." That was how it should be.

"Really?" Will asked.

Matthew smiled. "Definitely. You just have to practice. I've had a lot more years to get fast, but if you work at it, you'll get better. I promise."

Will smiled, and Matthew climbed out of the pool, grabbed a nearby towel, and headed to the table, where Lucas and Rachel were huddled over her tablet. "Do you recognize anyone?" Matthew asked.

"No."

"Okay." Matthew pulled a chair over. "Look for people with their phones or cameras. Mostly people were playing and paying attention to their kids." Matthew pulled the tablet closer. "Like these people. They are definitely not who you're looking for." He lifted his gaze. "The Meijer store has a machine where you can make larger prints. I'd do that and then maybe eliminate the people you know aren't the ones. I took a ton of pictures, so if this guy was there, he's in one of them. The kids were all over, and I love landscape shots."

"You have a real eye," Rachel told him. "Some of these are gorgeous. Like coffee-table-book worthy."

"Thanks." He smiled and looked closer, then switched to another picture. "Check out this guy. He's got his phone out here… and in this picture too." He showed it to Rachel. "Maybe if you make it bigger you can get more detail."

Rachel nodded slowly. "I have a better idea. I can hook this up to the big screen in the room. That will give us more than a print. Do you need me here right now? The area is still closed for another hour." Brianna and Carl came over, shivering. Matthew got towels and wrapped them up, then sat them in chairs with some Goldfish and juice boxes.

"Get everything set up, and I'll call you when we're ready to come up."

"And I'll make sure the hotel clears the people away from the doors." Rachel left, and Matthew returned his attention to the kids, not even realizing a crowd had gathered outside the pool doors.

Matthew wasn't sure how he felt about a bunch of strangers watching him and Lucas with his kids. But Rachel seemed to be taking care of things, as people from the hotel ushered everyone away. Sure, there was going to be talk about where they were, but at least they weren't going to be gawked at.

Lucas's phone rang, and he answered it and paled slightly. He listened and then hung up.

"We should get the kids back to the room and dressed. There are posts over social media, along with pictures of me, at the hotel. People are going to be swarming around this place soon." He sighed softly. "Maybe I should just go back to Hollywood."

Matthew felt a touch of panic well up from his belly. "It'll be the same there. Besides, this is your hometown." Matthew's jaw set. "And people should treat you better." He got the kids together and wrapped in towels. Then he gathered everything, and as soon as Rachel returned, they went down the largely empty halls to the suite.

Rachel took Brianna to help her change, and Matthew got the others dressed and settled at the table in the room. Lucas was a lifesaver and ordered hot snacks from room service, which fascinated the kids. They stayed near the door, trying to listen for the server who would bring the food.

"Take a look at this," Rachel said. Matthew joined her and Lucas in the living room, with Carl climbing on his lap. Brianna ended up on Rachel's, and the others sat at the table, playing surprisingly quietly while they waited for the food.

Lucas leaned forward. "What am I supposed to be seeing?"

"Check out the guy right here. This is the man Matthew pointed out. He's holding a camera through all the shots, but I don't think he's our guy." She went on to the next picture. "I think he's taking pictures of his wife and kids. You can just see them at the end of this picture."

"Okay."

Matthew stared at the images, not sure what he was looking at. "Him," he said suddenly. "Go back." He pointed. "The man in jeans and the black shirt, turned to the side. It was hot as heck today. Why would anyone dress that way? Unless you got a call and raced out to try to stalk someone."

"Let me see if I can find him in any of the other pictures," Rachel said and slowly went through the rest of the images.

"There," Lucas said. "He's, like, taking a picture straight into Matthew's camera." He got up and went closer to the television. "I don't remember seeing him before. Do you?"

Rachel shook her head. "What I'm going to do is go through all of the images we have from the previous case. There was a lot of security camera footage as well as the photos outside the various events that he was at. Let's see if we can't put a face to this guy, and from there, we can get a name." She continued moving through the pictures, but no one else stood out to Matthew or to Lucas, not that Matthew expected it. He could only look for someone who seemed out of place. Beyond that he was of little help, and that was frustrating. Matthew wanted to be able to do something.

Room service arrived, and Matthew got the kids settled at the table with plates and cups. They munched and talked as they ate. Matthew took a few bites and watched Lucas. By the time everyone was done eating, Carl was dozing off on his lap, and Brianna was most definitely flagging. She probably wouldn't nap, but a little quiet time was definitely needed.

"I think it's time for us to go. I need to pick up the van and then get something at the store for dinner before getting them home." It had been quite the eventful day, but now he needed to get the kids settled in for the evening and make a small dinner before bath and bedtime. Then maybe he could relax a little.

"All right," Lucas said, and they gathered their things and went out to the SUV. Once again, Rachel drove. Matthew paid the repair bill at the garage—which didn't stretch the budget too far, thank God—before transferring the car seats back to their places and getting the kids inside.

It was quiet behind the garage where the van was parked, and Matthew had all the kids inside. "Thank you for everything." Matthew swallowed. He was sure Lucas would have plenty of things to do, and this felt like goodbye. It was too much to expect someone like Lucas to want anything more with a guy who had four kids. It had been good to see Lucas again and to know that the kids hadn't completely killed his libido, but whatever fantasies he had about Lucas were just that, and it was time to return to reality. "It was wonderful to see you again." He didn't know what else to say.

Lucas nodded. "It was," he whispered softly, his eyes warm and kind of mushy. At least that was what Matthew thought, and seeing that familiar expression brought back old warmth. "I missed you."

Matthew quirked his lips. "I bet you were so busy you—" He squeaked slightly when Lucas drew closer.

"I mean it. I thought of you a lot." Lucas tugged Matthew even closer and then kissed him.

Matthew closed his eyes and for a second was transported to the time when Lucas first kissed him under the bleachers after band practice. The world fell away and then returned with a snap. Lucas backed away. "I'll call you, okay?"

Matthew nodded absently because he couldn't really think straight. Then he got into the van and started the engine for the drive home, thankful that the kids seemed half asleep, because he did not want to answer questions, especially when it came to Lucas, because he just didn't have the answers.

CHAPTER 5

LUCAS WAS grateful once the memorial service finished. He had made some sort of peace with his father, but that didn't wash away the years of hurt. It dulled them, though. Lucas had wondered sometimes what this moment would be like and whether he would feel anything at all.

"Are you okay?" Aunt Rose asked as they got up to leave the chapel at the funeral home.

"I will be," he answered. He didn't want to sound cold or cruel, but it was hard for him to bring up a well of emotion for someone who had written him off years ago.

Aunt Rose nodded slowly. "You know it's okay to be angry with your father and to resent him. What he did was wrong, and I think he regretted it. But don't let that be the only thing you remember about him." The sun shone on Lucas as the two of them wandered through the peace garden behind the building. "Try to remember the fun times when you were both happy, before your mother passed. Those were the good years. Let the rest go."

He nodded, knowing he would try, but it was hard not to carry it all with him.

"Lucas," Matthew said as he and the four kids approached. "They said you were out here."

"We wanted to make sure you were okay," Will said, his eyes downcast. He rubbed his cheeks, and Lucas took a deep breath, remembering that he wasn't the only one hurting.

"Thank you. How are you doing?" He looked at Will straight on. "It's okay to feel bad. That's what happens when we lose someone."

Will sniffed. "It feels like losing Daddy and Mama again." Lucas didn't know what else to do, so he hugged him, letting go of his own hurt, at least for now, to comfort someone feeling worse than him.

"I know it does." He lifted his gaze to Aunt Rose over Will's shoulder. "Just remember the good times and how they made you happy. The fun things you did together. That's what really counts." His aunt smiled and brushed away a tear as Will held him in return. Matthew seemed to have his hands full. "Do you know what makes me feel better at times like this?"

"What?" Will asked.

"Pancakes. Lots of pancakes. And ice cream."

"Yeah?" Will asked, and Lucas nodded.

"How about we all go get some?" There was a lunch back at Aunt Rose's church, but he hadn't intended to go. There would be too many people, and his stalker might try to make an appearance.

"Are you sure about this?" Matthew asked, adjusting Carl's weight from where he lay with his head on his shoulder. "This is a small town, and it's all over that you're here. I even heard on the radio that you're going to be on one of their shows." Matthew drew closer, and Lucas's attention fell on his plump lips. "Everyone is watching out for you."

"I know."

"So why don't you come back to the house and I'll make you pancakes? I also have ice cream in the freezer, along with fruit and sprinkles for Brianna."

"That's a great idea, and I can help you," Lucas offered.

Matthew laughed. "You mean you learned to cook since tenth grade, when you burned water and filled the school kitchen with smoke at least three times?"

"Har-har," Lucas groused, because he couldn't argue with the truth.

"And who taught you to cook?" Matthew asked.

Lucas cleared his throat. "I'll have you know that I've cooked with some amazing chefs." Matthew rolled his eyes. "Okay. I've watched my personal chef make things for me."

"That's more like it. And yes, you can help me in the kitchen." Matthew set Carl on his feet when he started to squirm. Then he took Lucas's hand. "You can do the dishes, but you'll have to wear gloves. I don't want your next director complaining that you have dishpan hands." Matthew took Carl's hand again. "We'll meet you at the house. And tell Rachel she's welcome too. Brianna keeps asking about her. I think she likes having another girl around."

"Of course. We'll be there soon." He found Rachel watching people, and they went to the car and escaped before people could gather.

"Are you sure this is a good idea?" Rachel asked. "There's no way I can provide security if people start showing up." The hotel had tightened its security and was only allowing registered guests inside, so yesterday one of the news organizations had booked a reporter into the hotel, and she tried to corner him. She had been summarily shown the door.

"Yes, I'm sure." He sat back as she drove. "I need...." He wasn't sure how to finish that sentence. "I'm tired of being cooped up in a cage of my own fame and notoriety. I want to see people, and Matthew is—"

Rachel continued driving. "Special?" she supplied.

"Yeah. He is. You've met a ton of famous people, and I'm not asking you to speak out of turn, but how many of your clients would ever consider raising their sister's four kids?" He turned to face her, and she gripped the wheel tighter. "See? He's amazing, and I let him get away. I don't want that to happen again."

"You want to see where this goes?" She shook her head. "You have to go back to Hollywood in a few weeks. What are you going to do, take all five of them with you?" Rachel suddenly stopped talking.

"Go on. You were never quiet or shy about your opinions. Don't start now. It's one of the things I like about you. Everyone else tries to tell me what they think I want to hear. You give it to me straight."

"Yeah, but someday you may fire me for my big mouth." She pulled to a stop at the light at Stiles Road before turning left, heading out toward Matthew's home.

"So you're saying I should just walk away." He had wondered about that himself.

Rachel slowed down. "I'm not telling you what you should do, but whatever it is, just make sure you know what you're doing." She pulled the car to the side of the road. "All I'm saying—and I have no right to tell you any of this other than the fact that you're better than most of the other people I work for—just know that there's more than just what *you* want at stake here. Those kids will grow to like you, and Matthew... well, he's a good, kind person."

"And it's been a long time since I had someone like him in my life," Lucas admitted softly. "Maybe you're right, and—"

"Or maybe I'm wrong," Rachel interrupted. "Hell, it's possible I don't know shit about anything. All I'm asking is that you think through what it is you want, because soon enough, you're going to return to Hollywood and get back on the treadmill for your next movie." She grew quiet and pulled back onto the road.

Lucas sat back, trying to clear his head. "I know, but...." He sighed. "I can tell you this because I know it won't go any further, but...

I'm fucking lonely." He leaned forward, tugging the seat belt with him. "I haven't had anyone give a rat's ass about the real me in years. The studio is only interested in how much money they make and how many people I can pack into a theater. My agent wants his cut, and everyone else just tries to see what they can get from me. But Matthew, he doesn't want anything from me. He never did." Lucas swallowed hard. "He was the one person who loved me for me, and I left him behind." There was no other way to put it. "I know I was a kid and it was years ago. Maybe I'm just being stupid, or I could have finally figured out what's really important."

"Or your mind could be going in a million different directions because you just went to your father's funeral. Just give yourself a break and a chance to breathe. Don't make any rash decisions." She slowed and pulled into the gravel drive, then up to the ranch house. Lucas got out of the SUV, but Rachel stayed inside, checking her phone.

"Son of a bitch," Rachel growled, half under her breath.

"What is it?" Lucas asked before he closed the door.

"Just get inside and stay there. I need to arrange for a different car. It seems that your damned stalker was at the service today. There are pictures of you and the car." She got out, leaving the car running, and approached him. "Will you be okay here without me? I'd really like to trade in the car and get a different one."

Lucas chuckled. "Too bad we don't have someone to drive this one all over town to confuse this guy." He really wanted to make the man's brain explode.

"That isn't a bad idea. Let me make a few calls and then I'll be in." She got back in the SUV, and Lucas went to the door. He knocked, and Brianna opened it with a smile.

"Hello," he said brightly.

"Where's Rachel?" she asked. Clearly she had bonded with his security detail.

"She'll be back later, okay?"

Brianna nodded. "I drawed her a picture. I wanna be a kick-butt lady just like her." She closed the door behind them and turned toward the kitchen before yelling, "Uncle Daddy, Mr. Lucas is here."

"Why don't you take me to him?" He held out his hand, and she took it and led him into the kitchen. Matthew was already making batter, with Will carefully getting fruit ready. Gregory was whipping cream as fast as his little arms would let him. Even Carl had a job. He was putting out the silverware. Lucas wondered what someone was going to do with three spoons or two knives, but Carl was working so intently that Lucas didn't want to say anything.

"How can I help?" Lucas asked.

"Why don't you find something on television? Brianna is finished with her chores, and Carl is almost done."

"So am I," Gregory said as he intently continued whipping the cream in the bowl.

"Where did you learn to do that?" Lucas asked, staying out of the way in case Gregory lost control of the bowl.

"His class did a unit about eating balanced meals, and they had a class breakfast. Their teacher showed the class how to whip fresh cream." Matthew smiled as Gregory began to flag. "That's really good. Why don't you help Lucas find something to watch?" Matthew stood at the stove with a griddle on the burners. Will put the bowl of fruit on the table and fixed the silverware before heading into the other room.

"This looks really good," Lucas said softly as Matthew turned toward him. He drew closer, glanced at the doorway, and then tugged Matthew to him, kissing the man hard. Damn, this was everything… even better than what he remembered. And it felt so right, like Matthew was the other half of himself.

"Lucas, I…," Matthew whispered, and then kissed him again, still holding a spatula. Lucas pressed their bodies together, wanting to take Matthew down the damned hall and lick him all over. But that was out of the question. He gentled the kiss and pulled back just as Matthew snagged another quick kiss.

"I saw Uncle Daddy and Mr. Lucas kissing," Brianna announced in a whisper that could probably be heard for miles.

"Brianna," Matthew scolded with a sharp edge to his voice. She had the decency to lower her eyes and appear admonished. "You know how I feel about tattling." Brianna nodded and then went to play with the others. "Sometimes…." He turned back to the stove without finishing his thought.

"You just want a few minutes to yourself?" Lucas finished.

"Yeah. And I know today has been hard for them, but it has for me too. Your dad was good to us. I know you didn't get along, but he was a different person lately, I think."

Lucas pulled out one of the chairs. "Tell me about him." Lucas mainly remembered the arguments and butting heads with the most obstinate man on earth. He had been so wound up in his own beliefs that Lucas had had no choice but to get away from him. They hadn't spoken since he left, with only Aunt Rose letting him know about the family. "Did he know about you?" Lucas rolled his eyes at himself. "Of course he did." It had been his father finding him and Matthew together that had set off the fight that had torn the last shreds of their relationship apart.

"He did. But he also knew the kids, and when their parents died, he sent over things for them. Your dad was lonely, I know that, but he was good to the kids and then, by extension, to me." Matthew poured batter on the grill to make the first pancakes. "I think after a while the whole gay thing meant less to him than spending time with us."

"Did you ever talk about me?" Lucas asked.

"No. I tried a few times, but I was met with that brick-wall stare of his, so I let it go. Adam used to come over a few times a week. He'd have dinner with us and play with the kids. Each Friday night, he'd come over and shoo me out of the house so I could have some time with friends. He and the kids would watch movies. They loved their Grandpa Adam, and I grew to know him… in a way. We didn't talk about you and me being gay or what had happened between the two of you. Those subjects just didn't seem appropriate." Matthew flipped the pancakes and turned around.

Lucas had so many questions, but it was clear he wasn't going to get the answers he might have hoped for. "But I can tell you that a few months ago, I had a date… of sorts." He actually seemed to blush. "It didn't turn out to be much, but your dad looked after the kids."

"And he knew?" Lucas asked.

Matthew nodded. "Loneliness can change a person." He went back to his pancakes, and Rachel strode into the kitchen. "What's going on?"

She turned to Lucas. "I spoke with the office, and they are going to send someone to back me up. We have a job in Detroit that is ending, so Haven Marshall is going to drive up here with a new vehicle. He'll park it at the hotel, and then he'll use the one we have to try to see if he can lure out the person who's watching you."

Lucas glanced at Matthew, keeping his voice low. "What about Matthew and the kids? I'm worried that my being here will put them in the line of fire, so to speak."

"Haven is going to stay here in town as added protection. Judging by the pictures that have been posted, your stalker only seems interested in you. At least that's the focus of his images." She was all business and stood straight and tall. "I wish I had more answers than I do."

"The house next door is empty, and the drive goes around the side of the house. The old owners used to work on cars in the back. The SUV would be out of sight there."

Rachel nodded and left, returning just as Matthew set the plate of pancakes on the table and called the kids in. Brianna left a place for Rachel next to her, and they all sat down to eat. Matthew helped Carl make up his plate, with Will seated next to him, taking his first bite of pancakes with syrup. They shared a smile, and Will nodded. "See, I told you. Pancakes make it better."

"Is Grandpa Adam in heaven with Mommy and Daddy?" Gregory asked after he swallowed a huge bite of pancakes.

"Yes," Matthew answered, his voice rough. Lucas lightly patted his leg under the table, and Matthew took his hand. "They're all together and watching over all of you, like guardian angels."

"And Grandpa Adam doesn't hurt no more?" Gregory asked. He was the shyest of the kids, but there were times when his insight was astounding.

"That's right. So remember the good times you had with Grandpa Adam, like when he came over with ice cream and you all watched movies together."

"Or the time he took us to the arcade," Will interjected. "And he always had birthday presents for us, even when it wasn't our birthday." He took another bite of pancake as Lucas set down his fork. He hadn't known what to expect, but his father seemed to have had a whole life here with Matthew and the kids. A piece of Lucas wished he could have been part of it.

"It's okay to be sad," Will said next to him.

Lucas smiled slightly. "You're right." Lucas was sad, mostly for the lost time and the fact that he never got to spend time with the person his father seemed to have become. Maybe that was the saddest thing of all, the missed opportunity—on both their parts—to patch things up and get to know each other as adults.

"But pancakes help," Will said before taking another bite.

"Yes, they do." Lucas ate a little more, but his appetite had slipped away.

Matthew squeezed his hand and then released it. "I hear you're going to be a guest on the radio."

Lucas nodded. "Yes. I contacted them. Aunt Rose in involved with a benefit for the pediatrics wing at the hospital, and she asked if I'd attend. They're having trouble selling tickets."

"I don't think that's a good idea," Rachel interrupted. "Not the interview, but attending something so public. You'll be announcing where you'll be to everyone." Her gaze grew firm, and Lucas knew what she meant.

"I'm aware of that. But I can't stay in my hotel room all the time, and Aunt Rose needs me. I won't let her down. Besides, I can do some good this way. People will buy tickets if they know I'm going to be there."

"Because you're famous?" Will asked.

"Yes. Some people will want to meet me because of that." He shrugged and bumped Will's shoulder lightly. "Being famous isn't all that important. It's what you do and how you treat people that really counts."

"We'll need to go over a security plan," Rachel said, and Lucas nodded. He'd expect nothing less.

"I want to help."

"I think it's a good idea." Matthew took Lucas's hand. "Remember, this is your hometown. People here have fond memories of you, and they are proud that you came from here. This isn't like LA. Tell them what you want. Be honest with them."

"What do you mean?" Rachel asked.

"Let the townspeople know that you're here and that you're excited about it and looking forward to meeting people at the benefit. Tell them that someone is trying to get too close and invade your privacy, or something like that. Everyone will understand, and they'll be on the lookout for anyone doing things they shouldn't."

"Are you kidding?" Rachel asked.

"No," Matthew told her. "When the last of Lucas's movies showed here in town, people lined up for tickets. It ran for weeks. They had 'hometown boy' on the marquee, and they do it for all of them."

"Huh," Lucas said. "I never knew any of that."

"If you want privacy, just tell people that you're here because your dad died. Most people will respect your wishes."

Lucas turned to Rachel. "That's a good idea." She didn't seem sold but didn't offer any criticism either. "It isn't like I'm going to advertise where I am or what I'm going to be doing, other than the benefit. Getting the town on my side, respecting my privacy, rather than trying to see where I am, can only help."

Rachel nodded. "That's true."

"Can I be on the radio too?" Will asked.

"Yeah, can we?" Brianna asked.

Lucas smiled and turned to Matthew. "If it's okay with Uncle Daddy. I'm fine with them coming along to make a guest appearance."

Matthew thought about it. "As long as you promise to be good and do what Lucas tells you." He seemed happy, and the kids would have a good time at the station. It wasn't like they were going to have a lot of time to speak, but they could say a few words. It would be nice, and it would help promote the benefit. "Now finish your pancakes and have some fruit. Then you can all go outside to play for a while." Matthew looked tired.

Lucas finished eating and helped clear the table. The kids all trooped outside, and Rachel excused herself to make phone calls.

"I'm sorry about the kids."

"Why?"

"You don't have to take them all to the radio station. I can make up something about the station not being big enough or something."

Lucas began loading the dishes in the dishwasher. He was probably doing it wrong, but he wanted to help. "It's great if they want to come." He put the last of the plates inside and finished loading the silverware and glasses. Then he closed the door and sat at the table. Rachel was still outside on the phone, so they were alone when Matthew brought over two cups of coffee.

"You don't have to do all this. I know you're just being nice...."

Lucas looked deep into the bluest eyes he had ever seen. "I'm not doing anything." He leaned forward. "I never forgot you. Over all these years and the distance."

"Come on. There were gorgeous guys all over the place. I remember that costar you were rumored to be dating. He was handsome."

Lucas shook his head. "Henry and I never dated… ever. We went out a few times because we both needed someone to hang out with, but that's all. Henry had a very definite type, and I'm not it." He grinned. "Let's just say that Henry likes them really big. And that's fine. He and I were never going to be anything other than friends. Just like the other people I know."

Matthew sipped his coffee. "Why?"

Lucas swallowed hard. "Because I met someone who stole my heart years ago, and he never gave it back." He gently stroked Matthew's cheek. "I have spent the last fifteen years comparing everyone to you."

Matthew rolled his eyes. "How can you?"

"I notice you don't have anyone in your life. I know you have the kids, but there were a lot of years when you didn't." Lucas gently traced Matthew's cheek, and Matthew's eyes drifted closed under the touch. That was the vision Lucas had spent years seeing in his mind, the way Matthew looked when he touched him. No one ever gazed at Lucas that same way. "I missed you like a limb. I wish I had brought you with me. I can't tell you how many times I wanted to come back for you."

"But you never did," Matthew whispered.

Lucas shook his head. "Because I kept wondering if it was all in my head. Years had passed, and I figured you must have moved on by then, so it was easier to stay away." Part of him knew that keeping in touch was a two-way street, but with his privacy and the number of people around him, it would have taken a miracle for any message from Matthew to reach him. The reality of the situation was that he had to be the one to initiate contact… and he hadn't.

"So you were alone all that time?"

Lucas shrugged. "I am rarely alone. Most of the time I'm surrounded by people, but yeah, I was alone in that I didn't have anyone in my life a lot of the time." He took a sip of coffee. "And I have to be honest with you, even if you had come with me, it's doubtful you and I would still be together. I spent years building my career. That meant months on the road and in the studio. There were weeks when I didn't go home. I spent the nights in a trailer on the set. Early on I shared with other actors, but as my fame grew, I got my own trailer, but by then I usually had someone like Rachel sleeping in the other room. Either that or my assistant did in case I needed something. My days start at three or four in the morning if heavy makeup is required. I can even sleep in the makeup chair if I have to. Then I work until ten or eleven, grab a few hours' sleep, and get back at it. I traveled all over the world and saw very little of it outside of hotels and location shoots."

"I see. So there wouldn't have been time for me," Matthew said.

"I don't know. If you were there, I'd like to think that I wouldn't have worked so hard. But then it's doubtful that I would have the career I have. Though that's both good and bad." The simple fact was that Lucas couldn't go back to change things. He had made his decisions, and right or wrong, good or bad, they were what they were. "I know things would have been different...."

"And if I had gone, then who knows what would have happened to the kids after Eden and Jack died. So I suppose things did work out, in a way."

"Yeah, they did." Lucas took Matthew's hand. "And maybe this is our second chance." He squeezed lightly. "I really want to try to find out. I'm tired of being alone, and I'm just exhausted with looking for someone when the one person I know I want is right here." God, it would be so easy if he could simply decide to stay and make a life here. But that would mean walking away from his career and everything he had built. And if he was honest, Lucas wasn't ready for that. Still, he figured he'd work through things when they happened.

"I'd like that too," Matthew said softly, getting up to look out the window. Lucas did the same, watching the kids playing some version of tag out on the back lawn. "But I don't always get what I want. I have the kids to think about, and what they want and need has to come first."

"Of course it does," Lucas said, even as he wondered if that was something he could live with. He was used to being the center of attention, and he took it for granted sometimes. Still, kids had to come first. They were the ones who needed care and looking after. "And I would never ask you for anything else." If he had issues with that, then it was his problem to work out, not Matthew's or the kids'.

"I know that." He sighed slightly. "Let's see what happens, okay? You can't make promises any more than I can." Lucas sat with Matthew, just holding his hand. It felt like something they would have done in high school, and yet it was tender and gentle.

Matthew's phone dinged with a message, and he looked at it, smiling. Then he unlocked the phone, their hands slipping apart. "I have a regular poker game tomorrow."

"Then you should go. Who stays with the kids?" Lucas asked, and Matthew's eyes filled with sadness. "It was Dad, wasn't it?"

"Yeah. He'd come over, watch movies with the kids, and put them to bed. I never stayed out too late, but it was my one night a week out." He answered the message, and his phone dinged again. "Geoff says to bring the kids." He bit his lower lip.

"Then go and have fun."

"Do you want to go with me? Geoff is great about guests, and I can let him know I'm bringing someone." He seemed so excited, and it had been a long time since Lucas had had a guys' night out.

"Are you sure it's okay?" he asked as Matthew texted and received his answer. "If you're sure, I'd love to come with you." He grinned as Rachel returned. Matthew poured her some coffee, and she sat down to let Lucas know what was happening.

THE FOLLOWING evening, Rachel drove the new car to the address Matthew had given her. Haven was about town in the other car, and judging from what Rachel said about the social media buzz, the ruse seemed to be working. "Are you sure about this?" Rachel asked. "Do you want me to check the place out?"

"I don't think it's necessary. Did you scope them out online?" He knew she had, because she always did. "Then you know they have a horse-riding program for kids with disabilities and that Geoff and his partner are some of the most respected people in the area."

"Fine. But I'll stay close by just in case." She made the right turn onto Sugar Grove Road and then into the drive of a two-story farmhouse that had probably been there for nearly a century.

Lucas opened the door to get out. "I'll call if anything happens."

Rachel nodded as Lucas grabbed the bag of snacks. Matthew's van pulled into the drive, and he waited until Matthew and the kids joined him. If he was honest, Lucas had been a little nervous. Still, he pushed that away, projected confidence, and followed along with the others.

"Come on in." The front door opened.

"Uncle Geoff," Carl called as he raced forward to get a hug, with Brianna right behind. They all received them. "Where's Uncle Eli?"

"He's out in the barn making sure the horses are all set for the night. He'll be in soon. Adelle baked cookies for you if you want some." All four of them trooped through the house. "Hey, Matthew." They shared a hug as well, and Lucas damn near growled. He had no right to be jealous, but it welled up from inside anyway. "And this must be your guest," he added once they separated.

"Lucas Reardon," he said, extending his hand. "I hope I'm not crashing your party."

Geoff shook his hand. "I recognized you, and you're more than welcome. Please come on in. I have the table all set up." He led them into a side room. "Let me make introductions. This is Joey—he's one of our managers on the farm—my dad, Len; Tyler, a firefighter in town; and Alan, his partner." They each shook his hand with a smile.

"I love your movies," Joey said. "So does my husband. He says they're loud and have great music." He wrapped his arm around a slight man who came up next to him. "This is Robbie." He held out his hand a little to the right, and Lucas took it, realizing Robbie was blind.

"It's nice to meet you," Robbie said. "I'm going to finish up the monthly reports while you have your game." Joey bent down gently to kiss Robbie. "Come get me when you're done." He left the room, and Lucas took the chair he was offered. Matthew and Geoff sat as well.

"What about the kids?"

"They're with Adelle. They love her. She'll fill them with cookies, and she's got paper, crayons, and a movie to watch with them." Geoff shuffled the cards and then handed them to Joey, who shuffled as well and then dealt. The game was simple five-card draw, and for Lucas, it felt good to just be one of other guys. No one asked about movie stars or for stories of what happened on set. The guys talked about crop rotations and a fire call to the school that turned out to be two kids smoking in the bathroom and setting the trash can smoldering.

"How are the kids handling Adam's passing?" Len asked. He had gray hair and bright eyes. "I'll take two," he added, passing over his cards.

"As well as can be expected," Matthew answered quietly. "It reminds the older ones of losing their parents." He took three cards. Lucas took one when his turn came as everyone offered their support. It was good knowing that Matthew wasn't alone.

A slender man with slight gray streaks in his black hair came in and stood behind him, his hand on his shoulder. His eyes were amazing, and when Geoff turned to look at him, the look of adoration almost took Lucas's breath away. He wished he could study that look. "This is my husband, Eli."

"Uncle Eli, can we see the horses?" Brianna asked as she hurried up to him.

Eli caught her as she lunged for him and smiled warmly enough to heat the room. "Not tonight, honey. But you can come over sometime and you and your brothers can ride the ponies." She hugged him, and when Eli set her down, she hugged him again before running out of the room. Eli pulled up a chair and sat near Geoff.

"We can deal you in the next hand," Lucas offered.

Eli shook his head. "No, thank you." He touched Geoff's arm, and they both seemed a little happier. It was amazing how, without a word, their love shone like a beacon. "I don't play, not that there's ever much money at stake, but I can't bluff, and I never got the hang of cards anyway." Eli smiled and then gasped. "Hey, I know you. You're Superboy. Jake and I watched that together. It was good."

That seemed to break the ice, and the questions came quickly. Most of them Lucas had answered a million times. But Geoff's was the one that gave him pause. "What kind of life do you have with people always wanting a piece of you?"

"I love what I do, and being in films is an amazing job. But being famous—I hate that word sometimes—can make things difficult." He didn't want to sound like he was complaining.

"What would happen if someone came here to the house?" Joey asked.

"He'd make a call and the security that came with us would be here in less than a minute," Matthew answered before he could. "She's really nice, but believe me, no one wants to mess with her." He patted Lucas's knee. "Can we get back to the game? Lucas is here as our friend, not as a movie star." He shared a smile with Matthew, who squeezed his leg.

"How do you know each other?" Eli asked gently.

"Matthew and I were boyfriends in high school." Lucas took Matthew's hand. "He's the one I let get away." Lucas's belly fluttered as he held Matthew's hand.

"I always thought of *you* as the one *I* let get away." Matthew's expression was so soft, and he squeezed Lucas's hand before pulling away and clearing his throat. "I raise two dollars." Damn, Lucas loved how the color rose in Matthew's cheeks.

Lucas smiled at Matthew, squeezing his hand once again as the play thankfully continued. Lucas hadn't meant for so private a moment to have happened publicly. "Sorry," he whispered, and Matthew nodded.

"Uncle Daddy," Carl called as he hurried into the room. "There's someone in back." He hurried to Matthew and climbed onto his lap. Lucas called Rachel immediately to let her know.

"I'll check it out. Keep everyone inside," she said. "Lock all the doors until you hear from me. If you don't in ten minutes, call the police." She ended the call.

Adelle came in with the other kids, who clustered around Matthew. "Lock all the doors and stay away from the windows."

"I already locked up the back," Adelle said in her southern accent as Geoff hurried to the front. Then he pulled all the curtains and joined them at the table.

"I'm sorry," Lucas said softly. This sort of thing wouldn't be happening if it weren't for him.

"It's not your fault. That lies with whoever decided to wander onto my property." Geoff's eyes blazed.

"I'll get my rifle." Len leveraged himself up from the chair. He patted Geoff on the shoulder and went into the office. Lucas heard him talking to Robbie, and then he returned with his gun and sat back down, letting it rest on his lap. "If anyone tries to get in…."

A shot split the night. The kids jumped, and Carl began to cry as he held on to Matthew. Gregory came to Lucas, and Lucas lifted him onto his lap, holding Brianna's right hand while Matthew held the left. "I'm calling the police," Geoff said as Lucas's phone rang. He snatched it up.

"It's all right."

"What was the shot?"

"Some drunk idiot thought he was going to sneak into the barn to ride one of the horses, and he took a shot at me, then passed out. I have him here and will call the police. You might want to let the property owner know, because he's going to be the one to have to press charges. I have the situation under control." She was all business, and Lucas hung up and relayed the message.

"Were any of the horses hurt?" Eli asked, his eyes filled with concern.

"I don't think so, otherwise Rachel would have said something. Have you had troubles with drunks?"

Geoff rolled his eyes. "We get people wandering onto the property from time to time. With the college across the road, we sometimes get drunk students who decide a ride in the dark would be fun." He shook his head. "Three years ago we had a woman who decided that the horses needed to be free, and she opened every stall and pasture door. We spent hours locating all of the animals and getting them back." He patted Eli's hand. "It's going to be okay."

"I worry. What if someone wandered onto the property drunk while we're doing a therapy riding lesson?" He was clearly shaken up.

Lucas was relieved that this didn't seem to have anything to do with him and leaned back in his chair. Len left the room with his rifle, presumably to return it to the gun safe.

"Is the bad man gone?" Carl asked.

"He will be," Lucas told him in as gentle a tone as possible. "Rachel has him, and when the police get here, they will take him away."

Carl looked at Lucas with those huge blue eyes. "You promise?"

"I do. Rachel is really good, and she will keep the bad men away. I promise." He smiled, and Carl relaxed a little on Matthew's lap.

"Come on. Let's go see about another cookie," Adelle told them, and all four kids followed her. It seemed cookies trumped a strange man in the barn.

"I'm going to go check on things and meet the police. You all go on with the game, and I'll be back as soon as I can." Geoff left with Eli right behind him.

Joey gathered the cards and split the pot back to the players, but the mood to play seemed to have been broken. Robbie came out of the office, and Joey met him and took him gently into the living room. Len excused himself, probably to make a phone call. Matthew stayed at the table with Lucas.

"I'm glad Rachel was here."

"Me too. But I thought…." God, he didn't want to give voice to it. The past few days had been much more hectic than he had expected. Lucas had figured he'd go home, attend his father's funeral, and have a few quiet days. He should have realized that nothing in his life was so easy. "I'm sorry the kids got scared. That was the last thing I wanted."

"I know, and this wasn't your fault. In fact, having you here, and by extension Rachel, probably meant that the rest of us were a lot safer." He scooted his chair next to Lucas's. "Don't forget that I know you. Lucas, you always took responsibility for everything, even shit that was never your fault. This guy who followed you from California is a nutcase, and whatever he does is not your fault. It's his. I've tried to teach the kids that they are responsible for their actions, and I'm going to tell you the same thing. You aren't to blame for what a psycho does any more than Geoff is responsible for some drunk idiot wandering his farm."

Lucas leaned closer. "But what if this psycho hurts the kids trying to get to me?" He had spent the past couple of nights lying awake in his bed, wondering if he should just go back to California. Then at least the stalker would go with him. Matthew and the kids could go back to their lives, and….

"That's what Rachel and her people are for. You pay them to keep you safe." Matthew looked him deep in the eyes. "I can tell what you're thinking."

"And what's that?" Lucas asked, his skepticism showing.

"I know who you are. The real you, not the man on the screen. You're thinking that you should go home and everything will be okay. The stalker will follow you, and then the kids and I will be fine and our lives will be just like they were before." He quirked his lips slightly. "And maybe you're right and all those things would happen. Except then you'll be in California, and I'll be here, and some light I didn't know I was missing will be gone."

The ache in Matthew's eyes sent a stab through Lucas's belly. "I'm going to have to go back eventually," he said softly.

Matthew's eyes grew harder. "Don't you think I know that? Your life is there, and so is the career that you excel at. I can't expect you to stay here in this tourist-centered backwater. You have a gift that you have to share with the world. It's what you were born for." He was so genuine and caring. "But I was hoping for a little time with you. Is that too selfish? I love the kids, and I'd do anything for them. I'll spend the next decade and a half raising them. But right now, with you here, I need just a little time for me—for us."

Lucas understood what Matthew was saying, and he couldn't argue with him. "Let's see what happens."

Matthew sighed and leaned against his shoulder. Lucas put an arm around him, Matthew fitting perfectly against him the way no one else ever had.

"The police are here," Will said as he hurried back in. He didn't pause when he saw them, which Lucas took as a good sign. "Can we go see?"

"No. Stay in here. You can watch through the window, though." Matthew motioned Will over. "But you should look after Adelle and make sure she's okay."

Will stood straighter and nodded. Then he left the room, walking tall into the kitchen, taking the others with him.

"That was smooth."

"He wants to grow up so badly."

Lucas held him closer, just watching the play of the lights from the police cars on the ceiling. It wasn't too long before Geoff, Eli, and Rachel came in.

"They have him, and none of the horses were hurt," Eli said as he sat down on the sofa. "It's all okay."

Rachel nodded her agreement. "I'm going back outside now that the police are gone just in case someone else decides to pay a visit." She left, and the guys took their places at the table once more. They began playing, but the lighthearted mood of the evening was gone.

They played a few hands before Lucas's phone rang. Everyone tensed. "It's just my agent," Lucas said before getting up from the table to take the call.

"What the hell is happening there?" Leon Sanders snapped at him, setting Lucas's already jangled nerves on edge. "Why am I hearing about you being seen with some guy and his kids?"

CHAPTER 6

MATTHEW KNEW something was wrong; he could just feel it.

"What are you talking about?"

The distress and anger in Lucas's tone had Matthew on his feet. He peeked into the other room where Lucas paced the floor.

"Stop this right now. You don't get to talk to me that way. You understand?" Damn, the command in his voice was stunning. "That's better." Lucas continued pacing until he saw Matthew; then he motioned him over.

"What's going on?"

Lucas pulled the phone from his ear. "It's my agent. He's pissed because of the social media crap." He returned to the call. "None of it is that bad. The stalker from last year has snaked his way back to the surface, and he seems to be here. I have security." He listened once again, and some of the tension slipped from him. Still, Matthew was concerned. "The man in the pictures with me is a close friend from high school. ... We dated back then. ... Yes, he has kids." Lucas rolled his eyes. "Sometimes you can be such an ass, you know that?" He began pacing again. "This isn't just going to go away even if I come back, I hope you understand."

Matthew took Lucas's hand and just held it as Lucas listened to whatever his agent said.

"This isn't my imagination, so either help, or I can find someone who will." Damn, he was angry. "Good. Get the publicist on it if you feel it's necessary, but you keep Matthew and his family out of it. Do you hear me? Good. I'll call you in a few days." Lucas hung up.

"What in the heck was that about?" Matthew asked. "And what did he want with me and the kids?"

"There are apparently some stories circulating about the stalker, and there have been pictures online of you and me, so the entertainment press is having a speculative field day. Leon got his panties in a wad over it. His suggestion was to use the story as a way to promote my next movie. I put an end to that. I won't have you going through that."

"I see," Matthew said, relieved and pleased that Lucas would stand up for him that way. "I take it Leon...."

"Would sell his mother for good publicity or a movie deal. Leon is a good agent, but he's not the best human being." Lucas groaned as he lowered himself into a chair.

"And those are the kind of people you surround yourself with?" Matthew asked. "No wonder you're unhappy." He was willing to bet that these people tugged and pulled Lucas in a million different directions in order to get him to do what they wanted him to do. "I am glad you told this Leon character where to get off. That was pretty awesome."

Lucas smiled. "It was, wasn't it? Leon didn't know quite what to do when I let him have it. I don't think I've ever done that before. Maybe I need to do it more often. He seemed cowed after that."

Matthew checked the time and was surprised at how late it had gotten. "I need to get the kids home and to bed."

Lucas shoved his phone into his pocket. "Thank you for bringing me tonight. It was fun, and the guys were really great."

"Even with the drama?" Matthew asked.

Lucas rolled his eyes. "If you want to see drama, try spending eight weeks on a movie set. I've seen one of my costars chuck an iPad out of his trailer door because he couldn't get the music he chose to stop. Then there was the time that I was in a movie with a married couple who decided that they were going to split up in the middle of shooting. When the cameras were rolling, they were perfect, and as soon as the director said cut, the claws came out and they were cutting each other to ribbons. A drunk guy trying to sneak into a stable just doesn't measure up." He leaned closer. "I'm pretty resilient." Even Lucas's breath smelled perfect.

"I always knew I liked that about you," Matthew whispered.

Lucas nodded, closing the distance between them. He had been an amazing kisser in high school, and he had only gotten more proficient. It made Matthew wonder who he had been kissing, but then Lucan slid his hands over his cheeks, drawing him closer, deepening the sensation, and Matthew forgot about anything other than that single moment.

"Uncle Daddy and Mr. Lucas are kissing again," Brianna said.

Matthew refused to have his actions dictated by a seven-year-old, so he kissed Lucas once more before backing away.

"What have I told you?" Matthew scolded, and she looked appropriately chastised before leaving the room. "I need to get them home before they get overtired and have a meltdown."

"Sure. And I need to call my aunt and get details for the fundraiser. I also need to check in with a number of other people to make sure that plans haven't changed again." Lucas sighed, and the color drained from his cheeks. "To tell the truth, I'm not looking forward to going back. It's going to mean months of work with very little time off."

"I see." Matthew was starting to wonder why Lucas felt he needed to work this hard. His movies did very well, and he was famous and loved. People came to his movies because he was in them, which meant he had a huge fan base of his own. Still, it wasn't his decision to question.

Matthew got the kids together and thanked Geoff, Eli, and Adelle for everything. Then he got the kids into the van and said good night to Lucas before driving home.

"Are you going to marry Mr. Lucas?" Gregory asked.

"Why would you ask that?"

"Because you keep kissing him." Gregory was the thinker of the group.

Matthew didn't have an answer off the top of his head. "I don't think so. But Lucas and I like each other. Is that okay?"

"Yes. If you get married, I don't wanna be ring bearer. Carl can do that." Suddenly each of the kids had an opinion on what they wanted to be in a fantasy wedding sometime in the future.

"None of you has to be the flower girl or anything else you don't want to in my make-believe wedding that hasn't happened yet and probably isn't going to." He pulled into the drive and helped the kids out of the van. He had just gotten them inside when his phone rang with a strange number. "Hello?" He half expected it to be a telemarketer.

"It's Rachel."

"Hey."

"The hotel is overrun with reporters, and they all want to talk to Lucas. It seems someone called all the stations and told them Lucas was going to be making some sort of big announcement tonight. Now the parking lot is full, and I need to get him out of here."

"Then bring him to the house. You know where to park so no one sees the car, and make sure you aren't followed. I'll leave the front door unlocked because I'm going to put the kids to bed."

"We'll be quiet," Rachel promised and ended the call.

Matthew followed the kids inside and herded them down to the bedrooms. He helped Carl get undressed and into his pajamas. Then they brushed their teeth before he zoomed Carl into his bed. He shared a room with Brianna, and the two older boys each had their own room. Soon he was going to have to figure out a way to give Brianna her own room as well, but he had a year or so, he hoped.

"I love you both," he said gently, tucking them in and giving good-night kisses before making sure the night light was on. Then he turned off the overhead light, hesitating before closing the door. This was supposed to be Eden and Jack's job. They should have been the ones putting their kids to bed and saying good-nights. He turned away and then said good night to Gregory and Will before returning to the living room.

Lucas sat on the sofa, waiting for him. "Rachel is outside checking the perimeter."

"I didn't even hear you come in." He was a bit surprised, but then again, he had been intent on the kids. "Everyone is in bed, and hopefully they'll stay that way." He sat down, closing his eyes. "I'm so damned tired I can't stand it, and yet if I were to go to bed, I'd end up staying awake for hours."

Rachel came inside, closed the door, and locked it. "Everything is quiet. I called the hotel, and they said that they cleared everyone away."

"That's good, but obviously everyone knows where you're staying now, so it's going to be mobbed even more. Before it was social media, but this evening, the news teams had to report something, so they put the hotel and the fact that you were staying there on every damned station." Lucas was uptight as hell, and Matthew couldn't blame him. The entire situation was surreal as far as Matthew was concerned. "Is it so hard to ask for a little privacy? What are we going to do?"

"I'm working on it," Rachel said. "I'll figure it out in the morning. I already have a call in to the office for some additional help."

Lucas sat back and was quiet for a while. "What is this guy's end game? What does he want? Most stalkers are trying to get close to me. They want to meet me or to be a part of my life in some way. This guy is very different."

Matthew sat next to him. "How so?" He didn't understand any of this.

"Well, a lot of stars pick up a stalker. Their usual reason is they think that they should be friends, lovers, or they want someone important in their lives. It's often more of a nuisance than anything else. They show up to each appearance and try their best to be seen and get attention. Those are the most benign of them. There are the ones who take it too far and try to break into the house or try to get onto a movie set. They cross the line, and that's what my stalker did last year. He tried to get access to the studio on multiple occasions and made it to my quarters once. We didn't see him, but he left a note. It was then that I hired Rachel for the first time."

"What did you do?" Matthew asked Rachel, his mind starting to churn with ideas.

"I made a show of staying with Lucas, letting everyone know that they would have to go through me to get to him. After a week, the incidents stopped. I stayed on for a while, but nothing more happened. We figured he got discouraged and...." She shook her head. "When we looked into the incident where someone got to your trailer, the security footage was wonky, but we did get some. It didn't show much." She was already on her feet. "I'm going to have a copy of that sent over. Maybe someone from Matthew's pictures and that footage will match up—who knows? We had pretty much discounted its usefulness, so I bet no one thought of it."

"Don't call tonight," Matthew said. "Take care of it in the morning." He was already tired and had had enough excitement to last a while. "No one knows where you are, and the car is out of sight." He turned to Lucas. "Just try to relax, okay?"

Matthew got up and went to the linen closet. He returned with a couple of light blankets and a pillow for Rachel, which he placed on the far end of the couch.

"Lucas can stay here. I'll probably be up most of the night," Rachel said.

Matthew shook his head lightly and held out his hand. Lucas took it a little absently. "Lucas is going to be staying with me." He got up and led Lucas quietly down the hall, leaving Rachel alone in the living room.

"Are you sure about this?" Lucas asked once Matthew had closed the bedroom door.

"The kids are asleep in the next rooms, and they could come in because of a nightmare or because they need a drink of water at just about any time." He needed to make sure Lucas knew the reality of the situation. "Go get cleaned up, and I'll meet you back in here." He let Lucas use the master bath, and he cleaned up in the hall bathroom, making sure that the kids' mess was taken care of.

When he returned to the bedroom, he found Lucas under the covers, bare shoulders showing from under the light blanket. Damn, he was more beautiful and attractive than he had been in high school. Matthew got undressed to his boxers and slipped under the covers.

"Do you have any idea how many people would give their eye teeth to be where I am right now?" Matthew asked as he settled next to Lucas, sliding his hand over his chest.

"And do you have any idea how much I'm only interested in one particular person being with me?" Lucas asked, rolling onto his side to face him. Matthew swallowed hard as Lucas slipped his hand around the back of his neck before drawing him into a mind-stopping kiss. Damn, the man didn't just know how to kiss—he seemed to be able to use his lips to stop time and make Matthew's brain short-circuit.

Right up front, Matthew knew this was a bad idea. But as Lucas pressed him back, his weight and heat surrounding him, Matthew's reluctance evaporated like fog in the sun. Maybe it was the fact that he hadn't been with anyone in two years and he was so desperate that he would have said yes to just about anyone. No, that wasn't true. This had nothing to do with that and everything to do with the fact that Lucas was in his bed. Matthew had dreamed of this moment, and Lucas didn't disappoint him.

The energy that surrounded them was almost too much for Matthew to take. And Lucas was hot. Not like Michigan hot, but in-the-movies California hot, and that was saying a lot. "Is this okay?"

"Uh-huh," Matthew said before he could think of anything else, because it was more than okay—it was shout-it-from-the-rooftops amazing. Lucas's hands roamed, and his lips tugged on Matthew's, driving him out of his mind. Okay, so maybe it had just been too damned long, but at the moment it didn't matter, especially when Lucas slipped down under the blankets. Matthew's boxers slid down his legs, and then Lucas took him to absolute heaven.

"Lucas," he whispered. The last thing he wanted was for any of the kids to wake up, and yet this was too amazing to stop. He also wanted to see Lucas, and this felt like hiding. Matthew yanked the covers away and groaned softly as Lucas took him all the way, sliding his hands up Matthew's chest, tweaking his nipples just hard enough to send a jolt of energy surging up his spine. He whimpered as Lucas backed away and brought their lips together once again. "If you stop now…," Matthew whispered, his mind reeling.

Lucas got out of bed, and Matthew's mouth hung open, because he was getting up and Matthew wanted to scream. But Lucas put a chair in front of the door to keep it from opening. Then he turned around, giving Matthew a show of Lucas Reardon in all his amazing glory. Half the world would give anything to have Lucas like this as he closed the distance to the bed before climbing back in.

"Now it's just you and me, like it should have been all along," Lucas said, straddling Matthew. He held his arms as he gazed at him like the world didn't exist other than with him. "It was always you. I want you to know that."

"How can it be?" Matthew asked. "There are…."

Lucas sat back, and Matthew couldn't look away, even as his own insecurities and worries sprang to the front of his mind. "Who am I?" Lucas asked.

"Excuse me?" Matthew whispered.

Lucas huffed. "Tell me who I am, please. Just tell me."

"You're Lucas… the guy I went to high school with. The man I…." Matthew paused. "You're the first person I loved. It was you who showed me that I was worthy of being loved." And he had missed that when Lucas left. "You're the man who left a hole in my heart that's still there. The one who can make me smile with that goofy look you have when you think you've done something amazing." Lucas smirked. "Yeah, that one. And you're the one I wish…." Matthew stopped himself, because nothing could come of those old wishes. The ones where he wished Lucas had stayed or that Matthew had gone with him. Those were high school wishes and completely impractical. "It doesn't matter."

Lucas touched his lips. "Yes, it does, because I have those same wishes." He leaned down, kissing Matthew so deeply he wasn't surprised when his feet tingled.

"But…," Matthew breathed. "That was a long time ago, and things change. Everyone changes."

"Of course they do," Lucas said. "But you still see me. That hasn't changed. You always saw me even when my parents and the other kids at school didn't. I was the theater geek, the kid who could sing and dance. You didn't care about any of that." He stroked Matthew's cheek. "And you still don't. You saw me for me back in high school, and…." Lucas's voice broke.

"I still see you. I always have," Matthew said as Lucas lifted his legs and spread them with his knees. Lucas reached to the bedside table, tore open the packet he snatched up, and within seconds, Matthew breathed deeply, groaning as Lucas slid slowly into his body.

"And I see you," Lucas whispered, his breath tingling against Matthew's lips. "I always did."

"No one else did." In school, Matthew was largely invisible. He wasn't nearly as outgoing as Lucas, and yet, just like right now, Lucas always seemed to see him and knew just what he needed and how to make him feel like the center of the universe.

The first time he and Lucas had done this, it had been... well, maybe to say it was a fumbling mess would be generous. But they learned together, and as their connection deepened, so did the passion. This time, the years slipped away and the two of them were like teenagers again. There weren't any children, no years of loneliness and longing, and Lucas was here with Matthew, looking into his eyes, transporting him, if only for a little while, to a place where he could be the center of attention.

"I missed this so much," Matthew whispered, and Lucas ran his hands down Matthew's chest, touching him, making Matthew ache for more. This was not about something as basic as fucking... and he had had that. This was a connection, through Lucas's eyes, hands, and the rest of him.

"How long has it been since someone touched you like this?" Lucas simply held him in his eyes and in his hands. There was no other way to describe it.

"I guess since you," Matthew admitted, arching his back as Lucas kissed him hard. His entire body was on fire, and Matthew went with it, letting the heat and passion take over. There was no need to hold on or try to control things. This was Lucas, and he could give himself over. That was what he did, until the white heat got to be too much and he tumbled over the cliff into a release that stole his breath. But what amazed him was the way Lucas held him through it, as well as afterward, once the chair had been returned to its place and the quiet of the night surrounded them. It felt like Lucas would never let him go, and he could have that, at least for a night.

LUCAS WAS still asleep when Matthew heard Carl talking to Brianna. He got up and pulled on pants and a T-shirt before leaving the room. Carl sat up in bed and then climbed out. He was always his morning boy, waking up with a smile. Carl hurried to him for a hug while his sister growled and rolled over, pulling her covers along with her. When he took Carl to the kitchen, he found Will and Gregory in the living room, watching television with the volume on low.

"Can we have french toast?" Gregory asked.

"Sure," Matthew said, looking at the pile of perfectly folded bedding. Rachel was nowhere to be found, and he wondered where she went. "Was Miss Rachel here when you got up?"

"No, Uncle Daddy." Gregory got up and hurried to the kitchen table. He came back with a paper that flapped as he walked. He handed it to Matthew and sat back down so he didn't miss anything important.

Rachel had left a note saying that she was returning to the hotel and would be back soon. She didn't give any additional information, but at least he knew where she was and he could tell Lucas when he got up.

"Carl, go get your sister up."

Carl shook his head. "She hit me last time."

"I'll do it," Will said and left the room. "Brianna, it's time to get up before I eat all the bacon." He didn't even enter the bedroom.

Brianna bounded out three seconds later, looking like she was ready for a fight. "Don't you eat my bacon," she said, stomping into the kitchen. "Where is it?"

"I haven't made breakfast yet."

Brianna glared at Will, who shrugged. "It got you out of bed."

She sighed as though the weight of the male world rested on her shoulders, but Matthew had to give Will credit for knowing his sister so well. "All of you get dressed, and I'll make french toast and bacon. But you need to be quiet, because Lucas is still sleeping." He turned off the TV and headed to the kitchen while the kids trooped off to dress.

Matthew wasn't sure how quiet they were, but he got everything for breakfast ready and got the bacon in the oven before checking on Lucas. The jumbled bedding was pooled around his legs, with the most amazing ass on full display. Matthew went inside and closed the door before sitting on the edge of the bed. He couldn't help patting that perfect bubble butt. "The kids are up, Rachel is out taking care of whatever it is she needs to, and I'm about to finish breakfast."

"Okay." He rolled over, and Matthew leaned across and kissed him. A knock sounded on the door, and Lucas grabbed for the bedding to pull it up.

"I'll be out in a minute," Matthew called.

"Let me get up and dressed and I'll come out to try to help." Lucas kissed him before climbing out of bed. "I slept better last night than I have in months." He pulled on his clothes, and Matthew left the room, making sure there were no little eyes to peek inside.

After returning to the kitchen, he started making the french toast while Will got out the toppings.

There was a knock on the back door, and Matthew let Rachel inside. She seemed a little frazzled, and Matthew had her sit at the table and got her some coffee, along with a mug for Lucas when he joined them. "The hotel was a madhouse, but I checked us out and managed to get the luggage. Leon called and demanded that I get you back to Hollywood, but I knew you had commitments, so I went ahead and rented a house. It's in Haven's name, and he's taking the luggage there."

"I see," Lucas said in a tone that said he didn't mind.

"We'll get you over there later today and make sure no one is aware of where you are. It should be fine."

"That's good, but the benefit is tonight, and everyone knows that I'll be there."

"Haven and I will also go, as will two additional security people who will arrive in a few hours. They flew into Grand Rapids and are driving up. Haven is taking the lead on the event security, and I will be leading your personal security."

"Can we go to the party?" Brianna asked. "We can dance." She started humming and broke into her best dance moves. Will turned on music, and all the kids started dancing.

"I know you can, but this is a grown-up party. We can have our own party here."

Lucas cleared his throat. "I was hoping you'd go with me," he said. "I need a plus one, but with all the excitement, I...." He sighed.

"I don't know if I can. I've taken some time off work because of the funeral, but I have to go in this afternoon for a while to check on things. Adelle said that she would watch the kids for me." He picked up his phone and sent her a message. Adelle came right back to say that she would be happy to look after the kids and put them to bed for him. Matthew swallowed hard and thanked her.

I'll be there right after lunch, and you can go on to work, she messaged, and Matthew put his phone back in his pocket, made up the last of the french toast, and got the rest of breakfast on the table.

Matthew sat quietly while the others ate. So much was changing around him, and he wasn't sure how to handle it. He was going out with Lucas, and they were going to be seen together in public. The biggest thing was that he was going to get a night out on his own. An adult night out. He could count on both hands the number of those he'd had in the past few years, and almost all of them involved poker at Geoff's. "I just need to know what I should wear," he told Lucas, and received a smile as bright as the sun.

"WHAT DO you think?" he asked Adelle and the kids after he got home from work. "Is this the right tie?"

Brianna groaned. "No, Uncle Daddy. Wear the gray one."

Adelle smiled and nodded. "She has a good eye."

Matthew returned to his bedroom to change ties and put on his dress shoes. He hoped his suit didn't look too out of style or shabby. Still, this was what he had, and he got his tie on and checked that the rest of him was right. Then he left the room and looked out the front window. Lucas hadn't arrived yet.

"You all need to be good for Adelle, okay?" he told his four munchkins. "Do what she says and go to bed at nine. All of you. Will, you can read if you like, but you need to be in bed. There's pizza in there for you to heat up, and—"

"I got everything," Adelle said gently. "Don't you worry about nothin'. I made cookies and some of my famous macaroni and cheese. It's already in the oven heating up. You and Mr. Lucas go out and have fun." She approached him with those huge brown eyes of hers that seemed to see everything. Robbie always said that growing up in Mississippi, where she had been the housekeeper and his main champion, he could never keep any secrets from her no matter what. She straightened Matthew's tie and fussed with his collar.

Lights shone across the front of the house. "I love you all," he said before opening the door. Carl hurried over to give him a hug, and then Matthew stepped out into the night. A limousine waited in the driveway. Lucas got out, looking incredible in his fitted suit and red tie. He smiled, and Matthew kissed him before getting inside. Rachel sat up front next to the driver, and once they were both seated, he backed up the huge car and they were off toward town.

"This isn't keeping a low profile."

"Yeah, well, we figured that we'd make a heck of an entrance, and then the driver would drop us off where Rachel parked the car so we could head on back to Muskegon. We've already put out a story that I'll be heading back to LA, so hopefully people will follow the car and leave us alone."

"We can only hope."

Lucas shrugged and then leaned closer. "You look amazing."

"No, I don't. I look like some country bumpkin in a suit next to you." He couldn't get over how Lucas's clothes hugged his body in all the exact right ways.

"You do not. You look amazing." Lucas gently touched his chin to lift his gaze. "Part of this is attitude. I have seen guys in jeans and a T-shirt, both of which were two sizes too big, who looked stunning because they carried it off. It's all about standing tall and wearing the clothes. Remember that. There will be people who want your attention and want to ask you questions."

"What should I say?" God, he was starting to get anxious.

"Whatever you want to. You can answer or not answer. But just be genuine and walk in there like you own the damned place."

"You do that. I don't know if I can."

Lucas kissed him hard, pressing Matthew against the leather upholstery. "I'm nervous too, but I never let it show. Remember, you own the place. Confidence and strength are attractive and exude power. And when you feel neither, just fake it till you make it."

Matthew nodded. It was only one night. He could keep it together. Lucas's aunt would be there, as would a number of other people he would know. At least that was likely, so there would be plenty of people for him to talk to.

They pulled up in front of the Marshall. A group of patrons had taken over the hall a decade earlier and restored and transformed it into the premiere event space in the area. Matthew peered out the window to where a group had gathered. They clapped, and the energy outside ramped up. The driver got out and came around to open the door. Then Lucas got out to applause and cheers from the crowd. He waved, and then Matthew climbed out and did the same.

Lucas gently held his arm as they walked toward the front doors. People did indeed shout questions, mostly to Lucas, and Matthew smiled and did as Lucas told him, standing straight and tall.

"Are you and Lucas dating?" someone asked. Matthew ignored the question as they got closer to the doors.

"Is Lucas paying you to come with him tonight?" someone else yelled, the question causing a buzz through the crowd.

"Of course not. Lucas and I are old friends." He smiled as people took pictures of the two of them.

"Matthew was my first boyfriend in high school. We reconnected a few days ago," Lucas said easily from next to him, smiling for the cameras, but as soon as Lucas caught his gaze, the smile shifted, and the cameras snapped wildly. Lucas leaned closer, his lips parting, and Matthew thought he might kiss him. Instead, he stayed still for a few seconds. "Always leave them wanting more."

Matthew laughed gently, and then they went inside. "Why did you do that?"

"Because they'll see whatever they want to, so if we give them something, they'll write about that. This way, we gave them something, but it's what we control." He took Matthew's hand.

"Okay," Matthew said as Lucas's aunt glided across the floor in a dark blue floor-length gown.

"Lucas. Thank you for coming." She hugged him gently. "Everyone is here, and we have the local press and radio station. We sold every ticket, thanks to you and that interview you did."

"Where do you want us?"

"I have places at a table for you up front." She led the way, and Matthew kept a hold on Lucas's arm, not willing to let him go. He didn't know how things like this worked, but he wasn't going to be left behind. "Dinner will be served shortly, and then there'll be dancing. Be sure to look over the silent auction table. I was hoping you might say a few words after the hospital president makes his appeal."

"Of course," Lucas agreed. "If that's what you want."

She was so excited. "A lot of these people bought tickets for the chance to see you."

Matthew could tell that Lucas wasn't thrilled. His smile was still bright, but Matthew knew it was pasted on. "I brought something for the auction." He reached into an inside suit pocket and pulled out an envelope. "I have a letter signed by me, as well as one of the pendants that I wore in the flashback scene from *Superboy*."

"You were always so sweet." She stroked his cheek and he squeezed Lucas's arm. Rose then hurried away as the hair on the back of Matthew's neck stood up. He turned around to check out what was behind him but saw nothing. Still, an uneasy feeling crept over him, and he wasn't sure why.

"We should sit down," Lucas said, taking his place.

Matthew sat next to him. "Hello, I'm—" He was about to introduce himself when a man interrupted him.

"My wife here is such a fan." He grinned, and the woman next to the guy in his midforties began gushing with the force of a fire hose. Lucas smiled and listened to her go on.

"Chopped liver," Matthew continued to himself as everyone's attention focused on Lucas.

"This is Matthew," Lucas interrupted, squeezing Matthew's hand. "He's a dear friend. He and I went to high school together." For a second, the smile warmed.

"So what was it like to be able to fly?" one of the other people asked as though what they saw on the screen was real. Matthew did his best to let it go without rolling his eyes. They weren't interested in him—or Lucas, for that matter. Only the illusions perpetuated by Hollywood, and who was he to break their fantasy bubbles?

The unease swept through him once more, and Matthew leaned close to Lucas. "I think your stalker is here. I keep feeling like someone is stepping on my grave. I don't see anyone acting weird, but this feeling won't go away."

Lucas nodded and squeezed his hand once more, this time harder as his gaze shifted slightly. Matthew followed it and saw the person Lucas did. He stood off to the side, phone in hand, which wasn't unusual, but his attention was riveted on Lucas rather than on the plate in front of him… or the person next to him, who seemed to be trying to get his attention.

"Would you like a picture with Lucas?" Matthew interrupted and pulled out his camera. "Why don't you lean close?" He got up and in a second snapped a group picture, as well as one of the intense man across the room. "If you give me your numbers…," he prompted, and texted everyone the picture. He also sent the one of the man to Rachel and got a quick response.

Excellent. Send any more you get of anyone you think is suspicious. I'm watching too, but I can't get as close.

I will, Matthew sent and slipped his phone back in his pocket. Then he ate the salad in front of him. It was decent but not great. He noticed that Lucas picked at his, eating very little, spending most of his time talking and listening.

"Ladies and gentlemen," Aunt Rose said, using a microphone. "I want to welcome you all to this evening's pediatrics department benefit." Polite applause followed. "We hope you enjoy dinner and the dancing to follow. The silent auction tables are in the back of the room, so please visit and bid often. All proceeds are for charity, and as a special treat, Lucas Reardon, who is with us tonight, has agreed to auction off the first dance of the evening. That's right, ladies—and gentlemen—who are interested, the highest bidder will have a spotlight dance with Lucas, so bid high and bid often. Enjoy the evening."

"Did you really agree?" Matthew asked, and Lucas shrugged.

"I honestly don't remember." He didn't seem upset, and there had definitely been a stir, with a number of people heading to the auction tables.

The servers took away the salad plates, while others fanned through the room with what looked like either chicken or fish, neither of which looked particularly great. Lucas's fish seemed like it was drowning in some sort of white sauce, and Matthew wondered if the poor thing should simply have been buried at sea. His own chicken was reasonably moist and not rubbery, if bland. Still, he was hungry, so he ate and listened as Lucas told a few stories about life on the set.

"What about something juicy?" the gushing lady asked. "I'd like a little gossip."

Lucas leaned over the table. "If I did that, then what kind of costar would I be? Your coworkers wouldn't like you talking behind their back, would they?" He said it with a smile, a wink, and a dose of charm, and she sat back.

"Quite right," she said, as though Lucas had gone up in her estimation rather than putting her in her place.

They talked through dinner, and Matthew did his best to keep up, but the conversation didn't really interest him. Once plates were gathered and dessert served, Matthew ate a few bites. Lucas ignored it. Then the head of the hospital got up to talk about the good work the donations gathered this evening would do. Finally Aunt Rose introduced Lucas, who walked onto the small stage to heavy applause.

"Good evening. You'll all be very happy to know that I won't be speaking for very long. This is a cause close to my heart. When I was eight, I broke my arm when I was visiting Aunt Rose. She took me to this hospital, our hospital, and they fixed me up so well that I was able to fly... in the movies, anyway." That got a laugh, and Lucas flashed a bright smile. Matthew knew that this was the performer in Lucas rather than the real him. His posture and his expressions were different. No one else would likely know, but he did. "This medical center provides lifegiving care to everyone in the area, and to its children in need, it's a lifesaver. Please give what you can." He stepped from behind the podium, a vision under the lights. "And please be sure to bid on the first dance, which I'm told will close in ten minutes." Lucas flashed another smile before descending the steps.

"You were really good."

Lucas leaned close. "I hate doing those sorts of things. I'm fine with a script, but if I have to speak off the cuff...."

"Fake it till you make it," Matthew handed back to him.

Lucas flashed a genuine smile this time. "Leave it to you to throw my own advice in my face."

"It's better than a glass of water. Now go ahead and circulate a little. Let people see you and meet you. I'm going to get us a drink, and I'll be sure to find you."

Lucas headed off toward some of the farther-away tables, saying hello and shaking a few hands. Matthew headed to the bar, where he waited in a group of a dozen or so people.

"Are you Lucas Reardon's date?" a male voice growled from behind him.

Matthew turned and came face-to-face with the man from earlier.

"Yes," he answered plainly before turning away, trying to keep from shaking. The man was scruffy up close, like he hadn't shaved recently. His beard wasn't even, and his breath smelled as though he had been drinking for hours. His cheeks seemed sunken, probably from the loss of a lot of weight, and his eyes were hollow. The scent of alcohol oozed out of his pores. His suit hung on him, like it was a couple of sizes too big. Everything about him seemed off. Matthew pulled out his phone and sent a quick message to Rachel.

"You know that isn't right," the scruffy man said.

Matthew tensed, wondering if he was in for some kind of homophobic rant. "What?" he asked, whirling around. "I really don't think your opinion really matters, do you?" He'd be damned if he was going to let some idiot get under his skin.

"He should be with someone better than you. Someone who really cares for him." The look in those hollow eyes was pure hatred, and it sent a chill up Matthew's spine. "You should stay away from him." He turned and began walking toward the table where Lucas stood.

Rachel made her way through the crowd, and Matthew caught her eye and pointed to the man approaching Lucas. She turned and made a beeline for him, but the creep saw her and headed for the door. Rachel went after him, talking into her radio, and Matthew joined Lucas, who looked up from his conversation. "This is Matthew." Lucas took his arm. "I thought you were getting drinks." He was completely oblivious to the incident and that Rachel was trying to get the man Matthew figured was the stalker. "Is everything okay?"

Now it was Matthew's turn to put on the smile. "It's great. I'll be right back." He returned to the bar line and got Lucas one of his dry martinis and a beer for himself. He returned and handed Lucas his drink.

"Thank you." Lucas leaned against him as he continued talking.

"Ladies and gentlemen, it's time to announce our first silent auction winner," Aunt Rose said, getting everyone's attention. Lucas downed his drink and went to join her. Matthew stood in front. "The winner is Anita Holden, who bid two thousand dollars." Everyone applauded, and Anita came forward. The music began, and Lucas glided her around the floor like she was a contestant on a dancing show. Anita looked great, but it was Lucas who held Matthew's attention.

The song ended, and Lucas danced with her a second time. Matthew took pictures for her as everyone in the room watched. When the second number ended, Matthew got pictures of them together and sent them to Anita, who was thrilled to get them.

"May I have the next dance?" a woman asked.

Lucas seemed about ready to accept, but then he said, "I promised to dance with my date." He swept Matthew into his arms and out onto the dance floor. Other couples joined them, but Matthew barely realized they were there. "Do you dance much?" Lucas asked.

"Just with the kids. I've been teaching Will to dance. Eden loved it growing up. She took a few years of ballet when she was a girl and some other dance classes later. It was important to her, so I want her kids to experience that. Brianna is really good, and she'll start ballet soon." When the music slowed, Matthew rested his head on Lucas's shoulder. There was something intimate and gentle about dancing. A silent heart-to-heart communication.

"And her Uncle Daddy is a good dancer as well." Lucas held him close, his arms around Matthew's waist. Part of him wondered if dancing with a man was going to cause trouble. This was a small tourist town in Michigan, and these people were not used to this sort of thing.

"Are people watching us?" Matthew whispered.

Lucas met his gaze. "I have no idea. The only person I'm looking at is you." They swayed in a circle, surrounded by other couples, and Matthew let his worries go, at least for now. He was here with Lucas in his arms, and that was his dream come true. When the song ended and another began, Lucas stayed where he was, and they kept dancing until Matthew lost all track of time.

LATER IN the evening, after Lucas's silent auction item had been awarded, they quietly left the party and got into the limousine, where Rachel was waiting.

"He got away," Rachel said as though she were swearing.

"I got a picture of him. Did you get it?" Matthew asked.

"I did and forwarded it to the team. Hopefully they can identify him. That was smart thinking, using the pretense of taking the group picture to get him on film, so to speak." She pulled out her phone and went to texting.

"Did you have a good time?" Lucas asked.

"I did. It was a fun evening." The best part was the dancing and the fact that Lucas had put everyone else off after he had done his duty. "Especially…." He swallowed, suddenly shy in front of Rachel. What he wanted to say was for Lucas's ears only.

"I know. It was nice having some time together. Everyone was good and happy that I took time for them, and they were so nice to give us space as well. I rarely get that."

Matthew slid closer, leaning against Lucas and closing his eyes, enjoying the ride.

As they approached the house, lights shone out front. "What the hell?" Rachel swore as the car pulled to a stop. "You all remain here, keep the doors locked, and do not get out." She jumped out and raced down the road like the hounds of hell were after her. Matthew watched as she waved her arms and began to yell. He couldn't hear what she was saying, but her tone was clear enough. Matthew cracked the window.

"You all need to get out of here now." She had her phone out. "Yes. I need the police, right away. I have trespassers that need to be taken in." Rachel was like a whirlwind as she spoke on the phone.

"We're the press," a man said.

Rachel got right in his space just before ending her call with the police. "You are on private property, trampling all over everything. That's destruction of property, and we will subpoena the film of everyone here as part of the charges as evidence. Do you understand me? I know plenty of people, and not the locals either. Let me call the federal district judge and we'll see what he says." Damn, she was something else. She got on the phone again, and apparently the reporters' phones started to ring.

They started getting into their vans and pulling away from the house as flashers appeared just up the road. The vans all stopped, and Rachel paused at the limousine.

"Let me handle this," she said.

"Okay. And I'll press any charges needed, so go after them with my blessing." The kids had to be scared out of their wits by now.

"Let's go while Rachel has everyone distracted," Lucas told the driver. They pulled into the driveway, and Matthew hurried inside.

The kids were supposed to be in bed, but all of them were in the living room, wired to their teeth, except Carl, who was in bed like he was supposed to be. "Okay, guys. The excitement is over and everyone is gone. Did you brush your teeth and everything?" Matthew was determined not to make a huge deal about this in front of them. If he did, he'd never get them to bed.

Lucas came in and got hugs from each of them. Then Matthew ushered all of them down the hall. They went right to bed. Now that everything was over, they were wiped out.

"Thanks, Adelle. I had no idea…," Matthew said.

"They showed up around half an hour before you got home. They knocked on the door and woke up the young'uns. I gave them what for, and they backed away from the house. I was fixing to call, but I had my hands full, and then you all got here. I didn't know what those people were gonna do." She was clearly rattled.

"You did right. Making sure the kids were safe and inside was the proper thing." Clearly the ruse of Lucas returning to LA hadn't held up.

She shook her head. "Those reporters were asking questions about you and Mr. Lucas. I told them to mind their own business and that their mamas would be ashamed of them for acting that way." She crossed her arms, and Matthew hugged her. "What's that fer?"

"Putting them in their place," Matthew said.

"Would you like to be the head of my press corps? I could use you in Hollywood. I swear all the reporters would be too afraid of you to get too close."

She waved her hand. "Go away with you." Adelle was clearly pleased at what Lucas said.

"If you want a ride home, the driver will take you," Lucas offered, and she thanked him and gathered her things.

"In that?" she asked, pointing toward the front.

"You ever ride in a limo?" Lucas asked. When Adelle shook her head, he grinned. "Then tell the driver you have the munchies and want to go into town. There's nothing like taking one of those through the McDonald's drive-through. Just don't keep the driver out too late." Lucas held the door, and Adelle peered outside before heading out. Lucas left with her and returned a few minutes later.

Lights flashed on the back side of the curtains as the limousine backed out of the drive. "What are we going to do? You know the reporters are going to be back one way or another, and I can't keep the kids inside all the time in case they show up."

Lucas nodded. "Let's get with Rachel when she returns and we'll figure it out. I promise." He was right there, heat washing off him as Lucas tugged Matthew to him. "I'm not going to leave you to deal with this on your own." He pulled Matthew into a hug. "We'll find the answer together."

Chapter 7

LUCAS KNEW the situation was becoming more complicated and that his problem was quickly becoming an issue for Matthew, and by extension his family. If he smoked, he'd probably have gone through at least three packs while sitting by the window watching for whatever happened next.

"Come to bed," Matthew whispered from behind him. He had taken off his suit and had on just a pair of light shorts and a T-shirt. Lucas had pulled off his tie and opened the collar of his shirt, but otherwise he was still in the clothes he'd worn to the benefit. "Nothing more is going to happen tonight, and staring into the darkness isn't going to help anyone."

"I know. Rachel said she was on her way back, and I wanted to know what she found out." He was getting more anxious with every incident. No one had said anything, but he knew that this had something to do with the person stalking him. He just wasn't sure how or what they wanted. The guy took pictures and followed him. Lucas suspected that he was tipping people off about his whereabouts and movements, but why? If the guy wanted access or to get close to him, then telling the world made no sense.

Matthew slipped his arms around Lucas's waist, resting his head against Lucas's shoulder blades. "I keep wondering why the press came here," Matthew said softly.

"Me too." Lucas put his hands on Matthew's.

"They seemed pretty intent on getting some sort of story, and just because you're here doesn't mean there will be one." Lucas slowly turned around. "I know we're a small town, and having a big movie star here has a lot of tongues wagging, but you've been here for a while, and people have seen you. That story is over."

"Okay…," Lucas agreed. Matthew had a point. Unless Lucas did something outrageous, there shouldn't be legions of people trying to follow him.

"So what was the cheese? The bait? They had to be tipped off by someone, but with what?" Matthew shivered. "One of the people outside the benefit asked if I was being paid or something. I ignored the question because it didn't deserve an answer. But what if that's supposed to be the story?" His eyes filled with pain. "Do they think I'm some sort of rent boy?" He began breathing heavily. "God, if that story is being reported, I'm going to have Child Services and everyone else at my door. Investigations, the kids' lives upended." He began to shake, and Lucas held him tightly.

"That isn't going to happen. I'd have heard if that kind of story were circulating. Leon would be having puppies—hell, man-eating puppies—if that were the case." Instead, he had been quiet, which was almost as curious. "I'll call my publicity people in the morning and see if anything is happening and what's being said." As far as he knew, there had been a few pictures on social media, a few speculations, but nothing more than that. People speculated about him all the time, and Lucas had learned to ignore it.

"But something is happening. I can feel it. There are things we don't know. Doesn't it drive you crazy? How can you live like this?" Matthew asked.

Lucas sighed. "To tell you the truth, most of the time it's no big deal. I have an assistant who helps me on set. Karen is really amazing, and she's been looking after the house for me and making sure that things in LA are moving forward. I have a driver when I need one, but I like driving myself. Rachel has been with me because of the asshole who won't leave me alone, but otherwise I lead a very busy but quiet life. I'm not one of those people who does outrageous things. I'm too busy. I put my energy into my work, not into making a spectacle of myself, so I'm not a huge target for the paparazzi because they can't get pictures of me, I don't know, trying to catch a greased pig or something."

Matthew laughed. "Did that really happen?"

"Yeah. Someone decided it would be a great stunt to promote their latest YouTube project. It wasn't pretty. The guys all missed, no one caught the damned pig, and it ran out on Melrose and got hit by a Mercedes." Matthew gasped. "Yeah, and the worst part was that the film was supposed to be about the evils of the pork industry or something like that. A don't-eat-bacon movie that killed a pig."

"At least they weren't trying to promote a version of *Charlotte's Web*," Matthew retorted, and Lucas chuckled gently. "Or *Babe*."

"Yeah. But the pig chasers were all known for crazy stunts, so their fiasco was all over social media for days, and everyone is always following them to see what they'll do next. That isn't me."

Matthew drew closer. "What *is* you? What do you do when you aren't working?"

Lucas sighed. "I'm always working. I think that's the problem. I've been working all the time for years. I have to be the most boring man in Hollywood. My schedule is so filled that the delay in starting my next film could impact the films down the line. I hope not, and I know that people will work things out because I can't be in two places at once. I also know that people like to work with me because I don't pull a bunch of crap and I'm a part of the team working to get the movie made. But I'm tired, Matthew. I had hoped that coming back home would let me rest and give me some quiet time."

"I'm sorry that hasn't happened. And maybe I've been part of the noise here—"

Lucas shook his head. "No. You and the kids are part of the quiet. Don't think anything else."

"How is that possible?" Matthew half snorted. "They are never quiet, and one of them always wants attention or needs something. Even when I'm in the bathroom, I can hear them chattering away, and half the time they knock on the door because they want something. Quiet they are not."

Lucas rocked them slowly from side to side, like they were dancing once more. "But what they want and say is genuine. There's no guile, no ulterior motive. And you... well...." Lucas was so tired of talking about his own life. Even in his head it came across as whining, and he certainly had nothing to complain about. "Let's just say that all of you make me feel real. The kids may talk and make noise, but it still leaves me feeling quiet inside." That was the best way he could describe it.

A car pulled into the drive, and Rachel got out, waved to the driver, and then hurried up the walk. The car pulled out once again, and Rachel quietly came inside. "I wasn't sure you would be up."

"I couldn't sleep until I had some answers," Lucas said.

Rachel pulled out her phone. "I wish I had more for you, but I do know a few things. First, the man from the benefit matched the man taking photos out at the state park the other day, but he doesn't match anything we have on the stalker from last year, which isn't a great deal, and we can't place him at any of the locations. We were able to match him to a driver's license photo. His name is Ralph Evers, and he lives south of Scottville."

"So two stalkers?"

"I don't think so. I believe we have a local fan who saw you at the park, and I believe he crashed the benefit, which was why he ran. Haven has already been to his address, and no one was home, but the place was lived in. Don't worry, we'll talk to him."

"Be nice, okay? If he is a fan...."

"I know," Rachel said. "But that leaves us with very little else. I plan to review all the pictures we have again. Somehow we must have gotten an image of our man somewhere. He isn't a ghost."

"Or maybe he is," Matthew said. "Obviously he's good at blending in, so we need to look at the details. If you want, we can do that in the morning."

"Is anything trending? Other than the benefit," Lucas asked, and Rachel stood straighter. "What is it?"

"I got to the bottom of tonight's little fiasco. It seems that someone called various stations with the tip that you would be making some sort of big announcement tonight. Then they gave the address here."

Lucas groaned. "Crap," he muttered under his breath. "Did they say what kind?"

"Something about your future. There was a lot of speculation among the reporters, but every station sent someone. I think they got a little overzealous when everyone showed up, like it reinforced the story...."

"When there was nothing to it," Lucas finished.

Matthew held him tighter. "Someone really knows how to manipulate the media."

"What?" Rachel asked.

Matthew pulled away a little, but Lucas still held him. "It's not like everyone knows the television stations or how to get their attention. They must get tons of calls every day, and yet whoever is behind this knew how to get through, created a juicy story, and got everyone here quickly. There aren't any television stations in town. Some of these people came from an hour away. That takes some slick talking and a knowledge of what will get their attention."

"True," Lucas said. "I wish I had thought of that."

"I doubt our guy from tonight is that media-savvy. I think he's an overexcited and maybe a little obsessive fan, but beyond that...."

"That would jibe with our stalker from last year. And he's using the same handle, Ruetoyou. It was dormant for a while." Rachel worked her phone. "Yup. Look here. The latest post. 'What's going on with Lucas Reardon? He's back where he grew up, and yet the press is still dogging him. What or who has he been up to, and how will it end?'" Rachel continued looking while Lucas seethed at the implication. Then his blood chilled. Was this a threat? "Jesus, there are pictures of the house."

Lucas pulled out his phone and checked the site. Sure enough, there were pictures of the reporters outside the house. "He was here, in that mess." Too damned close.

Matthew paled. "He was that close to the kids. And he put a picture of my house out there for everyone to see." He turned to Rachel, eyes blazing. "When we do catch this guy, I want first whack at him. I have kids, and he's putting them in danger with his craziness."

"Okay. Settle down, tiger. The first thing we need to do is make sure all of you are safe."

"I should be able to do that in my own home," Matthew said.

Lucas agreed. "I'll leave and make a big show of going somewhere else. Maybe that will draw them away." His first concern was that Matthew and the kids were safe. They didn't sign up for any of this.

"And put a target on you? No, thanks," Matthew said.

Lucas swallowed hard. No one fought for him the way Matthew was. "How big is this house you rented?" he asked Rachel.

"Haven got one of the homes on Hackett Lake. It has a private drive and plenty of bedrooms."

"If you want, move into the house with us for a while. There will be security, and the kids can swim in the lake." He sat down. "We'll need someone to stay with the kids when you're at work." Lucas sent a message to his assistant, and his phone rang seconds later. "I need a favor."

LUCAS DIDN'T sleep a wink. Every sound had him checking to see if someone was outside the house. Matthew was just as jumpy and anxious as he was.

As soon as light shone in the windows, Matthew got up and out of bed. Lucas rolled over and tried to sleep some more, but he gave up and dressed in his clothes from yesterday before finding Matthew in the living room, sitting near the front window.

"Are you sure we need to do this?" he asked.

Lucas's heart skipped a beat. "I don't know. I wish I had a crystal ball to know what is coming next, but I don't. The kids will be safe this way, and no one is going to know where they are." He perched on the arm of the chair. "Maybe it would be best if I left. At least then, the attention would leave with me."

Matthew turned his gaze on Lucas. "Is that what you want?"

Lucas shook his head. "We're way past what I want. This has little do to with that. You and the kids are more important." He sighed. "I thought I'd come back here to say goodbye to my father, spend a few days to help out Aunt Rose, and then leave town."

"And then…?" Matthew prompted.

"You know what happened then," Lucas whispered. "My first boyfriend walked back into my life with four kids, all of whom have me wrapped around their little fingers. But…."

Will shuffled into the room, still half asleep. "Hey…."

"Lucas has rented a house on one of the lakes, and he invited us to come stay there with him."

He nodded. "Is this because of last night?"

Lucas nodded, and so did Matthew. "There's also a boat, and we can all go out on it."

Will came closer. "Are you only inviting all of us because you want to spend time with Uncle Daddy? And what happens when you have to go home? Carl likes you, and so does Brianna. Gregory even talks to you, and he never talks to anyone he doesn't know. What happens to them when you leave?"

"Will," Matthew warned.

"No, he has a point, and he deserves answers." Lucas turned back to Will. "I don't know. I like your uncle and I always have, and…." Will deserved more than Lucas's doubts and an unknown future. "I wish I had a better answer for you."

Will shrugged. "I think no one has any answers."

"Do you want to go to the beach house or not?" Matthew asked.

"Do I really get to choose?" Will asked, and Matthew nodded.

"You're growing up, so it's time you make some of the decisions." Matthew stilled, and Lucas realized that he was watching one of those magical moments in life.

Will stood straighter and taller. "Okay. Then let's go."

Matthew chuckled. "Then go pack yourself a bag, and maybe you can help the others. We'll leave as soon as everyone is up and ready to go." Matthew waited until Will had left the room before slipping into Lucas's arms. "I should pack too."

"Don't forget your bathing suit." He hoped the words didn't come out as a growl.

AN HOUR later, everything was loaded into the vehicle, which Rachel had managed to keep out of sight. She hauled everything around the back and through the trees too, but Lucas still worried. She and Haven were coordinating the move, with him keeping an eye out for anyone who might be watching.

"We have everything. How are we going to get everyone to the SUV without being seen? We can't expect the kids to traipse through the woods, though they'd probably like it, especially Gregory. He is going through a phase where he loves bugs."

"Rachel has a plan." Lucas had to trust that she knew what she was doing.

"Okay," Rachel said after she came in the back door with the last of the luggage. "Lucas is going to make a show of leaving. Haven is bringing around the large SUV. You will get in and make sure you can be seen. Wave goodbye and everything. Play it up a little, but not too much. Then you and Haven will take off. After that, you get the kids out to your car. Talk about taking them to a friend's or something. Then head out. I'm hoping that Lucas is the one that anyone watching will follow. Take the kids through the drive-through, or to Nichols's Drug Store in town, even the grocery store. Make this seem like you're getting on with your life. Watch for anyone who might be following you. Then, once you've been out for a while, come to the house using a roundabout way. Here is the address and the code to get through the gate."

"And what about Lucas?" Leave it to Matthew to worry about him.

"Haven and I will get him there, along with the luggage." Rachel smiled. "We've done this before in tougher conditions. Though in LA we usually have traffic we can lose someone in. Out here, we'll have to be a little more creative." Lucas knew she was more than capable, so he did as Rachel asked and made a show of saying goodbye to Matthew in the doorway and then waving to the kids before getting in the SUV.

"Are you sure about this?" Lucas asked.

"Yes," Haven answered. "There's been a drone flying a little ways to the east. I believe it's probably got a camera. It never gets too close." He backed out of the drive and headed down the road toward town. About half a mile from the house, Haven pulled over and used a small cell-phone-like device, holding it out the window.

"What are you doing?"

"Sending a signal that's the same frequency as the drone is using to confuse it. If they stay away, there won't be a problem." He smiled. "It just fell out of the sky and into some trees because they got too close." He seemed pleased with himself. Haven raised the window and took off down the road, heading to US 10. He made a left at the corner, heading to Scottville. For a small town, there was a decent amount of traffic. Haven made a left again, passed through the north section of town, and once again made a left onto a small road. "I found a roundabout way to get where we need to be, and with all the tree cover, even with a drone, which is hopefully out of commission, whoever is trying to keep tabs on you is going to have a tough time."

The road was rough, so Lucas sat back, let Haven do the driving, and worried about Matthew. They were putting a lot of effort into his safety and using Lucas as the visible target, but what if they were putting Matthew and the kids in the line of fire with no one to watch them? God, he hoped this worked and that whoever was doing this thought he had left town and was returning to Hollywood. They'd be disappointed, and the ruse was only going to work for so long. But the hope was that by then, he and Matthew would have some time to themselves.

Haven eventually wound north to a major road. They hurried along before using a side road once more. This time, once they emerged, Haven took a quick right about a quarter mile down, entered a code at a gate, and they were inside. After waiting until the gate closed, Haven continued down the gravel drive and up to a large lake house. He pulled into the garage and lowered the overhead door. They had arrived and were out of sight.

"This seems like quite a place," Lucas said. "How did you find it?"

"The house is for sale, and we contacted the owners. They were happy to rent it out for a while. It was all done in my name, so no one is going to question it, or get very far if they do." Haven opened Lucas's door, and he got out. A car scrunched its way closer, and Haven opened the second door. Matthew pulled in, and then Haven closed that one as well. Everyone piled out of Matthew's car, and Haven led the way inside.

The house centered on a great room with a wall of windows overlooking the lake and the dock with a boat moored to it. The ceilings went up twenty feet, with an open kitchen and dining area off the spacious living room and a huge stone fireplace rising to the ceiling.

"Jesus," Matthew whispered. "This is some place."

"The bedrooms are up here," Haven said as he led the way upstairs, and Lucas left him and Matthew to sort things out. He wasn't needed for this. Instead, he found a coffee maker and got some started, because he was going to need it.

Excited laughter drifted down the stairs as Lucas settled onto the large leather sofa. It seemed the kids were pleased. Haven returned, pausing in the living room. "Thank you for all your help."

"It's no problem. I stocked the refrigerator and pantry. I'm going to change and go out for a run. I'm hoping I can check things out without anyone being the wiser. Rachel will arrive soon, but I won't be far, so call if you need anything." He went to the lower level, which Lucas figured he had set up as some sort of command post. Lucas was already tired and it was barely ten in the morning.

Matthew came down the stairs. "Everyone is all set and happy. There was a girl's room that has Brianna in princess land. Gregory has taken the smallest bedroom, and Will has the room with bunk beds to share with Carl."

"He looks after the younger ones, doesn't he?" Lucas asked.

"Yeah. Sometimes Carl gets scared at night. This way Will can be there for him. Gregory so much wants to grow up, so having his own room will be good for him." Matthew flopped down next to him, and Lucas gathered him in his arms. "I'm exhausted." He closed his eyes. "Is that coffee?"

"I made some if you want it. Though I was thinking I might try to get a little rest." After all, the house was quiet.

"Can we go swimming and out on the boat?" Will asked as he hurried into the room.

So much for a rest. "Yes. We can do both of those things. But first we need to wait until Rachel gets here with our stuff."

Will nodded as the other three tromped into the room. Matthew found a movie for them, and they settled in front of the huge television screen. Lucas went to find his bedroom, with Matthew following behind.

The room was huge, with a king-size bed, windows that overlooked the lake, and a private balcony with a hot tub. "This is nice," Matthew said quietly as he closed the door.

"Yeah, it is." He watched Matthew checking out the room, paying no attention to anything other than the way he moved. In some ways, it was like the years apart had never happened. Matthew could still make his heart race with just a look, and Lucas still wanted him—*needed* him, the way he needed to breathe.

But things had changed, and Lucas needed to be practical. There was a hell of a lot more at stake than just what he wanted. Matthew had a life here, and so did the kids. Lucas had a career in Hollywood, one that, despite its drawbacks, he loved a great deal. "I always wondered... I know you act, but have you ever written your own script for a movie?" Matthew paused in front of the window, the light making him glow a little.

"I've thought about it. I even have a few ideas." Lucas crossed the rough plank flooring to where Matthew stood. "One of the ideas is about us. A story of how hard it was in high school, keeping our secrets, how it ate at me that the one person who knew me best was the person I couldn't be honest about." He smiled.

"You were always honest with me."

Lucas nodded. "I was. I never told you a lie, and I shared my biggest dreams with you. But I was never honest *about* you. I kept my feelings from my family, and you had to do the same thing. As far as everyone in school knew, we were friends... but you were so much more than that." Lucas's throat threatened to close up. "It was Mason County Central, and our class was ninety-six kids. Everyone knew everyone else, and it wasn't the most tolerant place. You know that."

"I do. And I remember. I was lucky because Eden knew, and she would have kicked anyone's ass who gave me a hard time."

Lucas chuckled. "Yes, she would have. And your sister could use words like a knife."

"Uncle Daddy," Brianna called, "Carl is sick."

Matthew sighed. "I'm on my way." He squeezed Lucas's hand. "We aren't done talking about this."

"What? Our little depressing trip down memory lane?"

Matthew scowled. "No, your screenplay." He left the room, and Rachel came in.

"Everything went smoothly. Ruetoyou has taken the bait and posted that you're on your way back to Tinseltown with your tail between your legs—whatever the hell that means—so hopefully you and Matthew can have some time together. Haven is securing the perimeter. The kids have their luggage, but it seems that the little one ate something that his tummy hates."

"Is he throwing up?"

Rachel pulled a face. "No, thank goodness. Also, your assistant called. Her parents returned, and she's on her way. I assume she can be trusted."

"Yes," Lucas answered. "Karen knows plenty about my life that has never been reported to anyone. Give her the location of the house and have her park outside. Her car will be strange to everyone, and no one will think anything of it parked there." God, he hated that he was thinking like a security person.

"Okay, will do." Rachel paused. "And the kids are getting bored. The television isn't holding their interest when there's a whole lake out the window, glittering in the sunshine."

"And you want to go swimming too." He could see it in her eyes.

"Someone has to make sure the lake is safe and doesn't harbor any threats."

He really liked her. She left the room, and Lucas followed out to the living area. Lucas got some coffee and went through the refrigerator. Haven had thought of everything.

"Who wants Lunchables?" he asked, and Will, Gregory, and Brianna hurried over. He let them choose their favorites and set out juice boxes. Lucas got them seated at the table and felt pretty proud of himself. They were happy and eating.

Matthew came out with Carl in his arms, head resting on his shoulder. "His tummy is upset."

"Did you give him anything? Does he need anything? If so, we can get it," Lucas fussed.

Matthew lightly touched his shoulder. "I gave him half a Tums to chew, and I think it's doing the trick." He patted his back, and Carl let out a burp worthy of a truck driver. The kids snickered and giggled, and Carl began to squirm. "Do you want a Lunchables?" Carl nodded, and Matthew set him down.

"Juice?" Carl asked.

"How about some water to let your tummy settle? You can have juice later, I promise." Matthew got something for Carl before they each took a chair. "God, I'm tired."

Lucas was as well, but he figured he'd keep that to himself. Matthew looked worn out and at the end of his rope. His hair was all over the place, and the circles under his eyes only seemed to be growing. "Go on in and take a shower. Relax a little. Okay?"

Matthew yawned, covering his mouth with his hand. "I need to arrange for some things for the kids."

Lucas pulled out his phone and sent a message to Karen, telling her that they needed some toys and games. He sent the kids' ages to her, and she said she was already on it. Damn, that woman deserved a raise. "Go shower and relax. We can handle everything in time."

Matthew left, and Lucas leaned over the table. "So who wants to help me make some lunch for Uncle Daddy?" he whispered like it was a big secret. "He's really tired, so I thought it would be nice."

"What kind of lunch?" Brianna asked.

"I need to figure that out." Maybe he should have thought this through before he made the suggestion. "How about a salad with ham and turkey?" There was plenty in there.

Carl made a yuck face. "I don't like salad."

Lucas hurried around and tickled him lightly. "This is for Uncle Daddy. You already had your lunch. Okay?"

He nodded and giggled. Lucas didn't want to get his tummy going, so he let up and began getting things out for lunch. He gave Will and Gregory tasks to do, and gave Brianna and Carl a bunch of grapes to pull off the stems and put in a bowl. God, he was pleased with himself that he was getting the hang of this.

His phone chimed, and he picked it up and answered the call. "What's going on, Leon?"

"You sound in a really good mood," he said. Lucas refused to let his agent's grumps get to him. "What the hell has been going on there? Strange pictures and questions about you paying for a date?"

"Just someone stirring up trouble. One reporter decided to try to get a reaction from us and didn't succeed." He continued working with one hand. "Say nothing and all of it will die." He set aside the things he needed to cut and leaned back against the counter. The kids were happy, eating the last of their lunch and helping him.

Leon agreed, but he didn't sound convinced, which only got under Lucas's skin. Lucas had obviously given Leon way too much power over his career and too much say in what he did. All these years, Lucas had figured that Leon knew what he was doing and followed his advice. It had worked, and Lucas had prospered. But now something seemed off, and he couldn't put his finger on it.

"Okay. Then that's the plan."

"Fine. Where are you?" Leon asked.

"I'm still in Michigan. Everything is great." He wasn't going to tell Leon his exact location because he wouldn't put it past him to just show up. "There's nothing for you to worry about. I'll be back in plenty of time to start shooting." He smiled at the kids and rolled his eyes dramatically. They giggled at his expression. "Just relax and let me do the same. So unless there's something pressing…." He let the words hang there.

"Okay. Then we'll talk soon, and I'll set up some time so we can go over some additional opportunities."

"As soon as I get back," Lucas said and ended the call. He placed his phone on the counter, four sets of eyes on him.

"When are you leaving?" Will asked.

"Yeah… what's your plan?" Matthew asked, joining them. His hair was still wet, but he seemed more relaxed.

"I have about ten days. Then I'll have to go back and get settled again before I start my next film." Under normal circumstances, he'd be champing at the bit to get started, but for the first time in years, there was something else—*someone* else—in his life that he wanted just as badly.

CHAPTER 8

MATTHEW SWALLOWED hard. He had always known that Lucas was not going to be a permanent addition to his life. He had a career in Hollywood that he was going to have to return to, and Matthew's life—and the kids—were here. They all had friends and went to school here. This small town and the area around it was home, his and theirs. It was where he, Eden, and Jack had grown up. But he hadn't expected how empty he was going to feel once Lucas was gone.

"Can we watch TV?" Brianna asked. The kids seemed done with lunch, so Matthew got them settled in the living room and found a program they would all watch without fighting. Then he sat on the comfortable leather sofa out of sheer exhaustion and closed his eyes for a few seconds.

"Sweetheart," Lucas said, "I have your lunch."

Matthew opened his eyes and realized he'd fallen asleep. "Sorry."

Lucas set the bowl down on the table and left, then returned with one of his own before sitting next to him. "I figured you'd like something lighter for lunch. I found some ranch dressing, and I know you always liked that."

"Thanks," Matthew said, suddenly hungry. He ate the hearty salad and did his best to relax. Lucas leaned against him, and they ate together, watching the kids, until Lucas took their empty dishes back to the kitchen.

A buzzing cut through the quiet of the afternoon. Rachel sprang into action. "Your assistant has arrived," she told Lucas, who went out to meet her.

Karen was a little older than Matthew expected, with bright eyes and a smile that shone like the sun. He liked her on sight, and so did the kids, especially when she showed them the bags of games and toys she had brought.

"I hope it's okay. I got one of those big Lego sets. I figured it might be a way for all of you to spend an evening."

"It's a great idea," Lucas told her. "Did you have any problems?"

She shook her head. "Not that I noticed. No one seemed to be interested in me in particular. I drove right here and parked out in front of the garage as you instructed. I need to bring in my bags and stuff."

"I already have them," Rachel said. "I'll take them to your room."

Karen sat at the snack bar with Lucas next to her, and Matthew joined them. "What is it you need me to do?"

"It seems that my being here has stirred things up." He took Matthew's hand, and Karen pointedly noticed.

"I see. Good for you. I've worried about you working so danged hard all the time."

"The thing is, the stalker from last year is back, and he's made an appearance here in town. We're getting local posts under his handle, and we've had people planting fake stories and reporting where I am. It's been a little difficult. Matthew needs to go to work on Monday, and I was hoping you'd help with the kids. I have things I need to do to prep for my next role, and I can't exactly take them out to the movies or be seen in public right now."

Karen nodded. "Don't worry. I can get what you need, keep a low profile because no one knows me from Adam, and help keep them busy. Whatever is necessary." She leaned close to both of them. "You guys look exhausted."

"We had a visit from reporters yesterday after I attended a hospital benefit, and since then everyone has been on edge. My security people found this place, and I moved Matthew and his family here with us so they would be safe. We're all tired except the kids, who seem to have gotten a good night's sleep and are all energy."

"No problem." Karen left the room and returned with a cloth bag. "I brought lots of craft and art projects with me." She took the stuff to the table and started setting up. Brianna and Gregory joined her, and she got them started.

"She is a godsend," Matthew whispered. "I was coming to the end of my rope. I always promised that I would do my best not to yell at them, but…." He closed his eyes and finally allowed himself to relax once more. It was like a weight had been lifted from his shoulders, at least for a little while.

Carl hurried over to the table with the others.

"I draw too," he declared, and Karen included him. Will was the only one not joining, and he turned off the television and climbed into the chair with a book.

Matthew leaned against Lucas's shoulder. "What are we going to do about your stalker?" he asked softly. "Things can't go on this way. We can stay here awhile, but not forever. The kids need to go out, and I'm going to need to get them ready for school." He took Lucas's hand. "And you need to get this guy off your back. You can't go back to Hollywood and have this jerk tailing you." He needed to be found out, exposed, and dealt with.

"I'm not sure."

Rachel came into the room and perched herself on the edge of the chair across the way. "I have an idea."

Lucas tensed. "If it involves using Matthew as bait, forget it."

"The same goes for Lucas," Matthew added.

Rachel narrowed her eyes, and Matthew knew he had hit the nail on the head. "What we do is create a situation that's too good for our stalker to pass up. Then we put security people in the area to watch for him."

"But we don't know what he looks like," Matthew said. "How are we going to know who he is? If Lucas is going to be out in public, anyone could come up to him." He shook his head. "There has to be a way to catch this guy without putting Lucas in danger." He wasn't going to back down from this. No way in hell. "Wait," Matthew said. "We could stage something and trick them."

"How?" Rachel asked.

"On the south side of the river, toward the highway, is Pioneer Village. It's one of those recreated early settler places. We go there and take some pictures on the sly. We'd have to make sure we aren't recognized. We take the pictures, and then we get them posted the following day… as long as the weather is the same… saying that Lucas is there and that the pictures are live. We even get them to schedule a guest appearance of some sort. Maybe get them to go along in exchange for a donation. Get this guy to show himself."

"But how will we know it's him?" Rachel asked. "We've had multiple chances to identify this guy and have yet to do it."

"I know. But this time it isn't like we'll be taken by surprise." Matthew continued thinking. "Maybe you're right and we will need some bait. But we can use both of us together. Before, we were always trying to figure out who it was afterward. Something would happen, and we'd try to see if we could figure out what was behind it. This time we'll be the ones pulling the strings. You can have multiple people in the crowd watching, see who's taking pictures." Matthew grinned. "I bet if

Lucas were to do something attention-worthy, it would be too good for them not to post a photo. We'd need someone watching the feeds in real time to see if a picture gets published or when something is said."

Rachel sat back. "I get it. You and Lucas make a show of it. When we get a post on social media, we'll know where he is."

"Exactly. Then we can nail this guy down. Or better yet, someone can snap a picture of him."

"True. An identity would put us halfway to our goal." Rachel seemed excited, but Lucas's expression darkened.

"You can't put yourself in danger. Not for this."

Matthew shrugged. "Rachel and her team will be there, and I'll watch your back and you'll look after mine. Karen will be here with the kids, so they'll be safe and out of sight." It seemed like it was worth a shot. "It would also be a way for people to see their local celebrity. The Village, which runs on donations, will benefit."

Lucas growled. "I don't like this."

"Then we can all sit here behind gates and wait for someone to figure out where we are." He drew Lucas closer. "We have to try, if for no other reason than you need to feel safe and like your every move isn't being watched."

"True." Lucas sighed softly. "I'm getting really tired of being hounded. I just wish I knew what the hell they wanted."

"So you want to give this a try?" Rachel asked. "I know there are some risks, but we aren't getting any closer to bringing this to an end."

"Okay, we can try it. But I want enough people out there to make sure that Matthew is safe, and I'm going to need someone to stay here with Karen and the kids. I won't leave them alone… just in case." He crossed his arms over his chest. "I don't like this idea, but I also don't see any alternative at the moment other than doing nothing, and that sucks."

Matthew didn't like it either. The thought of putting Lucas in the line of fire made his stomach roil, but as far as he could see, if they wanted a chance to catch this guy, this was the only way to do it.

"ARE THE kids asleep?" Lucas asked that evening as Matthew returned to the living room after finally getting all four of them into bed. They were still wound up, but when he checked, even Will and Brianna were now sound asleep upstairs.

"Yes. For now," he said as he sat on the sofa. A flash of light illuminated the trees across the lake. "But I can't guarantee how long it's going to last. Carl will sleep through most anything, but Brianna hates storms, and it looks like we're in for one."

"Which means…?" Lucas prompted.

"That if she wakes up, it won't be pretty, and she'll probably have at least one of the others up as well." Matthew closed his eyes and sighed. Sometimes things just didn't work in his favor.

"I'm checking the radar," he said and pulled out his phone. "Oh crap," he said softly as more lightning flashed, this time brighter. "It's a line of storms heading our way from across the lake." He showed Matthew the image. At least the screen wasn't filled with red and yellow, which meant it wasn't going to be severe. Still, sometimes all it took was that first low rumble before Brianna was up and in bed with him.

The trees outside the window began to sway in the wind, and more lightning flashed, followed by the deep rumble of thunder. Lucas held him as they sat together watching nature's light show. As the storm drew closer, Matthew reluctantly got up and quietly went back upstairs.

The boys were still asleep, but as predicted, Brianna was awake and scared. What he hadn't expected was Rachel in the room with her. Brianna sat on her lap with Rachel rocking her slowly, telling her that everything was going to be all right.

"Uncle Daddy," Brianna said when she saw him.

"It's going to be okay. God is just going to make it rain, and he's being noisy." He stroked her hair, and Rachel continued her story. Brianna leaned against her, and Matthew silently thanked her. He got a smile in return and went to check on the others. Thankfully, they stayed asleep, and he went back to join Lucas in the living room and watch as the storm rolled in. Rain pelted the wall of windows, running down the glass for a few minutes until the wind died away. More lightning and thunder followed, but it was already growing quieter.

"It's just rain now," Lucas said.

Rachel came down the stairs. "She's back in bed and probably asleep again," she reported, pouring a mug of coffee.

"Thank you," Matthew told her. "What did you say to her? She's usually awake for hours."

Rachel sipped as she came to where they were sitting. "I just told her what a storm really was and how it worked. That the noise was just from the lightning making the air really hot until it makes a sound. Once she understood, she seemed to accept it and calmed right down. You have a really smart girl there." She nodded and left the room, leaving the two of them alone in the darkness.

"What are we going to do?" Matthew asked. "We're going to find your stalker and put that asshole out of business, or at least we're going to try. But what then?" His throat ached like it had been scrubbed with steel wool.

Lucas looked toward the floor. "What do you want to happen?" He shifted on the sofa, pulling his legs up, facing Matthew. "Don't tell me what you think is going to happen, but what you really hope will happen."

Matthew closed his eyes, not knowing if he dared put words to that. "I wish Eden and Jack were back here and that they could see their family and get to know the amazing kids they had. But we don't get those kinds of wishes." He felt tears welling in his eyes but refused to let them fall. "So I suppose that if I could get what I really wanted, it would be for you to stay with us. It's that simple. You'd come here to live, stay with us, and we'd all build a life together. I know you'd have to leave sometimes, but when you were done making movies, you'd come home to me." He sighed and kept his eyes closed, because if he opened them, the spell he was weaving would pop and reality would crash back in.

Lucas squeezed his hand. "You know that isn't practical."

"Yeah, of course. Nothing I want is ever practical," he snapped. "It never has been." He kept his voice low. "I always seem to want what I can't have." He turned toward the stairs. "Not that I'd give up the kids for anything, but...."

Lucas tugged him forward until he held him tight. "I know. When your sister and her husband died, your life stopped being your own. You gave up being Matthew and became Uncle Daddy."

"I did. Is it awful of me to admit that part of me resents that whole damn thing? They should be here to love and experience their children, and I should be free to go off and do whatever the hell I want. Maybe see the world, ride a camel in Egypt, or take a boat down a river in Europe to see all the castles. Maybe I could just take a night to get myself stinking drunk and forget about everything for a while, but I can't." Anger and resentment rose inside, and Matthew wished he could stop it, but it was too big and had been too long coming. He didn't want to feel this way.

"I have to be there for them, and...." He swallowed hard as shit he'd kept bottled up for way too damned long burst out of him like the storm breaking all over again.

Matthew hated acting like this. He had to be strong for the kids. They didn't need to see him like this. They deserved so much more than him blubbering like an idiot. He was only grateful that they were upstairs asleep.

"It's okay."

"No, it's not," Matthew said, inhaling Lucas's amazingly earthy scent. "I have to make sure they get through high school and college. They deserve the best life I can give them, and I intend to see they get it." There was so much pressure. He pulled away and wiped his eyes. "That's enough of the that pity party." He sniffed and blinked. He hadn't meant to break down like that.

"We all need someone to hold our hand every now and then."

Matthew held a deep breath, trying to clear his head. He closed his eyes, determined to get himself under control. "What is it *you* want?" Maybe if they switched subjects and got off the subject of him, Matthew could control himself. "What do you hope for?"

"Well, most people would think I have everything I could want. I have plenty of money, I'm famous, and I get to do the job I love most in the world. And to a large extent, they'd be right. But you've seen some of the darker side to what I do. I suppose if I could ask for one thing, it would be privacy."

Matthew tilted his head to the side. "Really?"

"Yes. I think if I could have some sort of life outside the public eye, then I might have a chance at what I want most." He held Matthew tighter. "But as much as I want a family of my own, I can't put them through that. You saw how it's been the last week." He sighed. "If I were to say what I want most, I'd say that I'd like all of you to move out to California. We could have a house of our own that overlooks the Hollywood Hills. The kids could go to the beach and have the best schools." For a second, his lips curled upward and his eyes danced with happiness. "That would be so nice."

"But what would I do?" Matthew asked. "Be the housekeeper? Your live-in booty call?" He had no place in that kind of world. "How much would you be away?"

"See, that's the hard part. I'd have long days at the studio, and you'd be home taking care of the kids. Then there are the times I'd be on location, and you could travel with me, but the kids couldn't be on the set. There would be nothing for them to do, and it wouldn't be fair to them. But if I could have anything I wanted, it would be you. I want you to know that."

"I think I understand," Matthew said. "You've made things pretty clear. In your world I'm the babysitter and houseboy sort of rolled into one."

Lucas groaned. "No. That's not what I mean. I'm trying to... I don't know, see how things would have to be. What I do takes a hell of a lot of time. Why do you think so many marriages in Hollywood break up? One partner can't take the separation... and can you imagine two people in the business? They spend most of the year on opposite ends of the world and never see each other. That's the last thing I want for you—for us."

Matthew blinked. "But you want there to be an us?" His heart leapt a little.

Lucas rolled his eyes. "Didn't I just say that? I do want there to be an us, you and me together. But I keep trying to see how you could be happy."

Matthew pulled back, his gaze heated and intense. "Isn't that something that I should be able to decide? Or isn't there room for us in your life? You want there to be an us, but you aren't willing to make room? How fair is that? You say you work hard and that you're busy all the time and travel a lot. Okay, I can live with that. But do you *have* to work so much? You're doing back-to-back movies and managed to pigeonhole a trip home to go to your father's funeral, and yet you have to be back in less than two weeks because you're scheduled to be on set again. Then you tell me that you have projects so backed up that a change in the schedule for one messes with the others. How can you have so little time? You say you want a family, but what would they have to do, call to make an appointment in order to get some time in your life?" He stared at Lucas.

"I think things got way off track here."

Matthew shook his head. "No, they got to the heart of the subject. If you want something badly enough, then you make room for it. It becomes a priority, and other things take a back seat. What it sounds like to me is that you want a family, but you want them to fit into your schedule that's already going a mile a minute." Matthew stood, his head aching.

"And you have all the answers?" Lucas asked, his gaze going to the floor.

Matthew shook his head. "I have very few of them, but that's something I know. The kids are important, so I make time. I work, yes, and then come home to them and spend all the energy I have on them because they're more important than me." He swallowed hard. "I guess what I really want, if I could have anything, is someone who puts me before themself… so I can put them before myself." Matthew turned and headed for the stairs. "I'm going up to bed."

MATTHEW DIDN'T know what think as he cleaned up and climbed into bed. He had really thought that Lucas cared for him. And he probably did. After all, he *said* he cared, and Matthew knew Lucas didn't lie or say things he didn't mean. But actions said a lot more than words, and Lucas not being willing to make room in his life….

Matthew groaned into his pillow. What the hell was he doing? They weren't making plans, and this was no ever-after situation. They had reconnected a week ago, and already Matthew was letting his mind race ahead. They had been talking wishes and dreams, and Matthew got carried away as usual.

He rolled over and figured he owed Lucas an apology. The guy must think Matthew had gone around the bend.

Footsteps on the stairs and then in the hall drew closer, and he closed his eyes. The bedroom door opened, and Matthew immediately knew it was Lucas. Maybe it was his scent or the fact that his pulse raced just because he was closer.

"Are you awake?" Lucas asked.

Matthew thought about ghosting him but rolled over. "Yeah."

"I'm sorry," he said gently.

"Me too. I got carried away, and…." He sighed and reached for the light.

Lucas stilled his hand. He pulled it back and slipped it under the covers, listening to the rain. He started slightly as Lucas slipped into bed with him, warm skin next to his.

"You only said what you did because it was how you feel." Lucas tugged Matthew to him. "You can always be honest with me. We don't have to agree on everything, and sometimes you'll be right and sometimes I will, but I always listen to you." He gently stroked Matthew's back. "We always heard each other."

Lucas was right. In high school Lucas saw him, the real him, and Matthew appreciated Lucas for the person he was. "I know that." He held him. "Do you have any idea how hard it's going to be when you go?" His heart was getting a taste of what he'd always wanted. Matthew had watched Lucas leave once before, though, and he was going to have to do it again.

"It's the same for me. Why in the hell do you think I work so much?" Lucas asked. "I have to do something." He kissed him, and Matthew groaned as Lucas pressed him against the mattress. "I've missed you since the day I left, and when I go back, I'll miss you again... only more. Before, you were a distant memory, something happy that I measured others against. Now you'll be sharp and full... something so close and yet so far away." He swallowed. "I don't know what to do."

"Maybe things will work out," Matthew told him, not really believing what he said, but hoping nonetheless.

CHAPTER 9

EVERY MUSCLE in Lucas's body ached, and yet he felt amazing. The sun shone through the windows, and reflective sparkles from the water danced on the ceiling.

"Can we go swimming?" Carl asked as he hurried into the bedroom with his bathing suit on backward and his floaties on his arms. He still had on his pajama top.

"In a little while," Matthew told him. "I promise. Now why don't you go back to your room and take off the swimmies and your pajamas. Then we'll have breakfast and go down to the lake." Matthew checked the time, and as soon as Carl left the room, he got up and dressed in a hurry. "I need to get him ready for the day, and I have to be at work in an hour."

"It's okay. Get him settled. Karen and I can take them down to the water for a little while." Lucas got out of bed and dressed, then followed Matthew, who headed right upstairs.

"But Uncle Daddy," Carl called and began to whine.

Lucas let him handle it and went into the kitchen, where someone had made coffee.

"You can go swimming," Matthew said, carrying Carl down the stairs. He now wore shorts and a T-shirt, all of which were on the right way. "But first you have to have breakfast, and then you need to ask Lucas, because I have to go to work soon." Matthew set Carl down, and he came right up to Lucas with those big sad eyes.

"Please…?" he asked, and Lucas had to work to keep from laughing.

"Of course we're going swimming later. But you have to let Uncle Daddy get ready for work. Miss Karen will be up soon, and after breakfast we can all go down to the lake for a while. Can you get your brothers and sister up?"

Carl raced up the stairs. "Get up if you wanna go swimming!"

"Are you sure you're up for this?" Matthew asked.

Lucas chuckled. "Are you kidding? They're nothing compared to diva costars and wannabes who think they're hot stuff. Let's get you something to eat and on your way to work." Lucas helped make breakfast and then said goodbye to Matthew, kissing him before he drove off.

"He's going to be fine," Rachel said, coming to stand next to him.

"I just hope he doesn't have any problems. Word is going to have gotten all over town about him and me." He was less concerned about the guys Matthew worked with than the press trying to follow him.

"Matthew can take care of himself, and I made sure he has all our numbers if something happens. Now, I think we need to get inside."

Lucas just hoped Matthew made it through the day in one piece.

"HOW CAN anyone do this day in and day out?" Lucas asked himself. He'd cleaned up spills and separated Gregory and Brianna, slathered all of them with sunscreen, and watched them do tricks in the water for what seemed like forever.

"Stay close to the shore," Lucas cautioned Will, who nodded. The last thing he thought he'd be doing on this trip was watching kids, and yet here he was with four of them all vying for his attention… in the best way.

"Carl can't swim yet," Brianna told him as she stood next to where he sat on the sand, dripping water all over. "But I can."

"Okay, but you need to stay close to shore." He had no idea what the kids' abilities were, but he was pretty sure that an eight-year-old was not going to be a strong swimmer, no matter what he wanted to believe. "We can make a sand castle if you want."

"A big one?" she asked, lifting her arms over her head.

"Sure. A big one." He got up and started helping the kids make a pile of sand. Will and Gregory came over, and soon they were all forming towers and the main part of the castle. Lucas helped dig a moat so the lake could fill it.

"Are you having fun?" Rachel asked as she strode over. Carl and Brianna nodded, barely pausing in their labors. She handed Lucas his phone, which he must have left inside. "It's been dinging constantly."

"Thanks." He checked the call log and groaned. "What's up, Leon?"

"John Kerrigan wants to meet with you. I can arrange it, but I think you should come back. That way you can meet him in person."

Lucas looked out over the water and let it calm him. He was not going to get caught up in Leon's dramatics.

"We can Zoom. It's fine. That's what he and I did the last time we worked together. I'm not going to travel hours for a twenty-minute meeting. Set it up and I'll meet him."

"But meeting him in person would be better. I'd think with everything that's happening out there, you'd be anxious to get home. We can control security here much better." He sounded so convincing— almost too much so.

"It's not necessary," Lucas said. "Just set up the call with John. It will be fine. He wants to go over his plan for the production and his ideas on my character. We can do that remotely, and it will free things up for him as well."

"I really think—" Leon continued.

Lucas wondered what the big deal was. "Why are you in such a hurry to have me back there?" he asked, cutting off Leon as he laid out his reasons for Lucas to come back to Hollywood.

"I'm not." The pause told Lucas that he had caught Leon off guard. "I just think it would be a good idea. You and John can meet and talk, and you'll be closer to where you can be protected. Who knows what kind of security they have there? It's the damned middle of nowhere. If someone is after you, then here you could have more backup and stuff." He paused. "Where are you exactly, anyway? Are you still in Scottville, or have you seen sense and left already?"

"I'm…." Lucas felt his ire rising, but he stopped himself. "I'm fine, and I'm safe right now." He grinned as the kids all worked together on their sandcastle. It was impressive, with Will taking the lead, explaining what he wanted the others to do.

"Are those kids?" Leon asked.

"Can you please just set up the meeting and let me know when it is?" He wanted to get this conversation back on track. "I'll be returning in a week or so. Until then, I'm trying to relax and get some energy back." He disconnected the call and wanted to chuck the phone into the drink just for a little peace. Was that too much to ask?

He shook his head, and Carl hurried over across the sand and sat on his lap. "You look mad. Was the man mean?" Carl hugged him, and instantly the anger slipped away. "If he's mean, then you shouldn't be friends with him anymore. That's what Uncle Daddy told Brianna."

"And he's right." Lucas wasn't happy with the job Leon had been doing lately. He'd been getting more demanding and pushy. Lucas hugged Carl back, and then he got up and hurried away to play with the others.

"Is there anything I need to know?" Rachel asked.

"No. Just my agent being a pain in the backside." He managed to stop himself from saying *ass*. "I don't know what I'm going to do."

She leaned down. "Are you sure that's how you feel?" He turned, because she was getting at something, and Lucas needed to look her in the eye. "I can see what I can find out about him. I never trusted Leon."

"Are you sure it's not because the two of you hated each other on sight?" Lucas narrowed his gaze.

Rachel shrugged. "I never hid the fact that I think he's a weasel." She leaned closer. "And what if my instincts turn out to be right? They have in the past." There were times when Lucas wished he wasn't surrounded by people who thought they knew better than him. "I'm willing to lay money on it."

Lucas leaned back, and the kids all grew quiet. "Okay." He nodded, and Rachel hurried off, probably to dig into the dark recesses of the web.

"Is she being mean?" Carl asked, his lower lip pooching out.

"No. Rachel is never mean. She's just fierce, like your sister is going to be when she grows up." Lucas grabbed a stick and a napkin from the snack bag and made a flag that he placed on the top of the sandcastle. "I think we should go in for a while." He was starting to wonder about their time in the sun.

"Can we have ice cream?" Brianna asked.

"Yes. After lunch, as long as you're good." He wasn't above bribery. With Will's help, he gathered everything and carried the bag and toys to the house.

Inside, the kids raced around in some dance of chaos centered on getting their suits off. Fortunately, Karen had made lunch, and once he got all the kids at the table to eat, he sat on the sofa, put his feet up, and wondered how anyone could do this each and every day. It wasn't like they were bad kids—it was just exhausting dealing with their normal behavior. Lucas felt grateful to every parent everywhere, and he'd only spent half a day at it.

"Is it good?" Karen asked, and Lucas listened as they all talked. He wasn't hungry, so he closed his eyes, trying to catch his breath.

A weight bounced on the sofa next to him. "When will Uncle Daddy be home?" Gregory asked, his blue eyes filled with mischief.

"Later this afternoon. He's at work now."

Gregory sighed and then leaned against Lucas. "I want Uncle Daddy."

"Aren't you having fun down by the lake?" he asked, and Gregory nodded. "Is something wrong?" Gregory shrugged. "You don't have to tell me if you don't want to." He sat quietly with him, hoping that just being there was enough. The others talked and ate lunch, with Karen watching them.

"Are you hungry, Lucas?" Karen asked.

He shook his head. "Are you sure you don't want to eat?" Lucas asked Gregory.

He nodded and sighed once more. "Are you going to take Uncle Daddy home with you?" Gregory asked.

Lucas held him closer. "Are you afraid he's going to leave you?" he asked. "Because that isn't going to happen. Matthew loves you very much, and he isn't going anywhere without all of you. I'm not here to take him away, I promise."

Gregory looked at him with big, watery blue eyes. "Really?"

"Matthew is your uncle, and he'll always be there to love you. I know that," Lucas said, his throat aching, because that was what he had hoped would happen for him. But it wasn't and it couldn't. As much as Lucas cared for Matthew and was coming to care for these four kids, they were more important than him. Matthew had told him that, but now it was finally sinking in. These kids had to come first, and Lucas needed to make the most of the time he had with Matthew, because this was going to be it. Lucas was used to getting what he wanted, but Matthew was someone he couldn't have. The kids and their lives here needed to come first.

"But he loves you too," Gregory said. Damn, these were amazing kids, and sometimes they just blew him away. Lucas hoped that was true, but at the moment, it wasn't what was important.

"Sometimes we can't always be with the people we love." That was so damned true it made his heart ache.

"Why?" Gregory asked with all seriousness.

"Because sometimes someone else is more important." He smiled as best he could. "Now, go on back and finish your lunch. After you're done, we can play games if you want."

"I have colors for you, and you can draw your uncle pictures," Karen offered, and Gregory went back to the table while Lucas stared out the windows. What he'd said slowly sank deeper. As much as he wished he could stay with Matthew, his life and his energy needed to be spent on the kids. As much as Lucas would love to ask him to come to Hollywood and stay with him, it wasn't practical. The kids needed stability and a routine. Lucas's life was anything but routine. Just like before, no matter how he felt, Lucas was going to have to leave… only this time he wasn't sure his heart was going to survive.

"UNCLE DADDY," Gregory called when Matthew came down the walkway from the house toward the water. All four kids stopped what they were doing and hurried over for hugs, clamoring to tell him what they had done. Lucas sat on the sand and gave the kids their time, watching Matthew.

The man seemed to have infinite patience, listening to each of them and giving hugs and big, warm smiles.

Rachel passed them on the walkway and came out to where Lucas waited. Her expression was as serious as a heart attack.

"I take it you found something," Lucas said as he got up.

"Maybe. I'm not sure," Rachel said, genuinely confused.

"Okay. Why not start at the beginning?" Lucas brushed the sand off his now dry bathing trunks.

Rachel showed him the screen. "It seems over the past few years that the number of clients Leon had under contract is shrinking, but his lifestyle…. Let's just say that it's expensive. Vacations, boats, a house in Beverly Hills as well as one at the beach in Malibu. All of which take a lot of cash to maintain." She showed him pictures of the various items. Lucas wondered where she got them but kept the questions to himself.

"Okay…."

Rachel looked at him like he was dumb. "Lucas, you're his cash cow. His other clients are somewhat successful, but nothing like you, and they don't bring in the revenue you do."

"What are you saying? That Leon is cheating me in order to live the life he has?"

Rachel shook her head. "I don't think so. You have an amazing team of business managers, and I'm sure they are on the lookout for anything like that." She bit her lower lip as Matthew slipped his arm around Lucas's waist.

"I think she's trying to tell you that Leon is working you like a dog so he can keep the money flowing in," Matthew whispered. "You already told me how tight your shooting schedule is. What sort of manager allows that and doesn't work to manage it? That sort of thing is part of their job, right? Yet he keeps you busy as hell and even bugs you when you're on vacation for a few weeks."

"So… what am I supposed to do? And how does this get us closer to finding the guy who won't leave me alone?" Lucas snapped and wished he hadn't.

Rachel lowered the tablet. "It doesn't." She seemed almost disappointed but recovered quickly. "But to that end, I made arrangements for us to try to set our trap for him on Friday. They are going to announce this afternoon that you are planning to make a special appearance at Pioneer Village to benefit their educational programs. Tickets will need to be bought in advance for the special event, which will happen in the evening, and they are limiting the number of guests. They asked if you would prepare a little speech about educational programs and how important they are to you."

"Of course."

"And how do we ensure that Ruetoyou is going to be there?" Matthew asked.

Rachel grinned. "I'm having one of the hackers back in the office who has been following this joker since you first hired us tweet it to him. Put the invitation right in front of his face. A small group with tickets open to the public—this is a stalker's dream. And we'll be there in the crowd as well. If anyone makes a move, we'll be on them."

"But how are you going to blend in?" Lucas asked.

"We'll be dressed in period costume and look like the players and volunteers. No one pays much attention to the employees at places like that. To most people, you become part of the whole setting."

"But how will you know him?" Lucas asked.

Rachel pulled up her tablet once more. "I think we might have pictures. I've had the team in the office going over every image we have, and look here." She pulled up one of Matthew's pictures from the day in the park. "See that guy right there...? Now look here." She flipped the image to a street in LA. "There he is in the background near the studio entrance. This was taken the day you received that note in your trailer."

"Why didn't we find this sooner? Not that I'm not happy you did, but...."

"Because the images aren't sharp enough for electronic comparison. Our eyes do a better job. We tried enlarging the pictures but can only get so far and get a huge number of possibilities. At an event with a limited number of people, though, we should be able to pick him out... if he decides to show up. All we can do is tease him and hope he takes the bait."

Lucas wasn't sure he liked this, but he was willing to give it a shot. "What do you think?" He turned to Matthew.

"I hate it, but I don't see where we have much choice. However, I am going to make a request. Since this is open to the public, let's stack the guests that are going to be there. Make sure we have as many friendly faces there as we can."

Lucas grinned. "What do you have in mind?"

CHAPTER 10

"ARE YOU sure this is a good idea?" Lucas asked, sitting up in bed, the soft light making a warm glow.

"What?"

"All of it?" he asked. "I don't know if I should go at all."

Matthew heard the fear in Lucas's voice and knew exactly what he meant. He sat on the edge of the bed in his boxers. "The thought of you doing this scares the crap out of me. And to make matters worse, all the kids could talk about was going to White Pine Village. They heard us talking and want to go too. I spent most of bedtime trying to explain that they couldn't." There had been plenty of tears, but there was no way in hell he was letting them anywhere near someone who was stalking Lucas.

"There has never been any indication that he's interested in anyone other than me, but you're right. The kids need to stay here. That way you'll know they're safe. We can take them for a visit before I leave, when no one knows we'll be there." Lucas stroked his arm to try to calm him.

"Adelle is going to come over that night as well, and Karen will stay with the kids. She's pretty amazing. I swear she can do anything." Matthew smiled. "Geoff and Eli, Joey and Robbie, and Tyler and Alan will be on the guest list. We can show them the picture of the guy we're looking for, and they'll be on the lookout as well. It would also give us additional support. Tyler is a firefighter, so he knows how to handle touchy situations, and he can easily call in a ton of backup if it's needed."

Lucas tugged him into a hug. "I can't believe you're doing this and that all your friends are willing to help."

Matthew leaned back to kiss Lucas. "Of course they would. These aren't Hollywood people who look out for themselves all the time. These are country folks. Eli and Geoff are some of the largest landholders in the county. Eli raises horses, and Geoff grows corn and has a large beef herd. They also have therapy riding for kids with disabilities, and Eli does that for any kid who needs it, regardless of whether they can pay." Matthew grew closer. "And everyone on that farm helps out. Robbie doesn't give lessons, but he spends time with the kids who have sensory issues, gives them someone to speak with. So yeah, they'll help. All I had to do was make a phone call."

"I see." He hugged Matthew tightly. "Maybe I've been gone way too long."

"Or maybe what you needed was some time at home with real people who show you who they are instead of fake ones who hide behind facades and make-believe." He leaned closer. "You always showed me who you were, and while I watched you on screen, it was the real person that made those characters come to life. It was the man under the costume that shone through each and every time. So the people here, my friends, your friends… all you have to do is ask, and they're there."

Lucas pulled him down onto the bed. "I think I'm coming to understand that." Lucas kissed him, and Matthew forgot about the rest of what he wanted to say. "I came to say goodbye to my father."

Matthew held Lucas's cheeks. "And I'm glad you got some peace between you."

"We did, and that was good. But what I didn't expect was what's been happening between us. I knew you were still in town, but…." Lucas paused. "I guess I expected my trip to last a few days and then I'd go back to California." He hadn't given it much thought when he'd originally left.

Matthew drew closer. "What is your life like out there? Do you go to parties and do glamorous things?" He smiled, and Lucas groaned.

"What's glamorous to you? Do I go shopping at fancy stores? No. Spend my afternoons having lunch with other stars in some exclusive café that takes months to get a table? No. I have a nice home with a beautiful view of the city. That's my one real luxury. I have a nice car, but it doesn't cost a fortune, and I drive it myself a lot of the time. The studio provides a driver when I'm on set, but when I'm there, I spend weeks in my trailer. So that becomes a home of sorts." He yawned and closed his eyes. "I guess my life is a lot of work and little else."

"Don't you have friends?" Matthew had talked to Lucas about his life, but he was still curious.

Lucas shrugged. "I know people out in LA. People I've worked with a few times. Occasionally I'll go out to dinner with one of them, or I get invited to parties. They're usually obligations, and I go because I need to make connections and talk to people. Some of them are pretty wild, and I stay for a while and then leave before things get out of hand."

"So you don't have people to watch television with and have a beer and some pizza? You know, those are your real friends. The ones who don't expect anything from you."

"Not really. There are times when I wish I did. But it's hard in a city of millions to get to know anyone when everyone is running so fast that they never have time to stop and meet anyone else." He shrugged. "I don't have that problem here." Lucas nuzzled Matthew's neck, and he once again forgot his train of thought.

"That's because we already know you…." Matthew's words trailed off into a groan as Lucas tugged him back. The heat of the day was nothing compared to the furnace that Lucas ignited inside him, making his ears ring. "Wait," he said gently, listening. Thunder rumbled in the distance, followed by feet on the stairs. Lucas backed away as Brianna and Carl hurried into the room and hopped onto the bed.

"Uncle Daddy, can we sleep with you?" Brianna asked, holding her doll under her arm. "Annabelle is scared."

Lucas snickered, and Matthew watched as he reached over the side of the bed, grabbed a T-shirt, and pulled it on.

"Are you and Lucas having a sleepover?"

Lucas got out of the bed and grabbed a blanket, but he paused in the doorway. Matthew wondered if he was angry, but he returned to the bed and kissed him gently. Then he left the room, and Brianna and Carl bounded up the bed and curled under the covers as thunder sounded once more. Matthew hoped the other two didn't join him; otherwise the bed was going to be very full. As it was, even with two kids, it seemed empty without Lucas.

MATTHEW WOKE, this time to the bed dipping more deeply. "What…?" he asked groggily.

"It's just me. Karen got up, and she and I carried the kids back to bed." Lucas had pulled open the sliding doors and let in the soothing sounds of the trickle of rain.

"I'm sorry about that," Matthew said.

Lucas slipped under the covers, right up next to him. "There's nothing to be sorry for. It's what you do for the people you love." He gathered Matthew into his arms, and he rolled over to kiss him. Matthew figured that Lucas would want to rekindle what had been interrupted, but he soothed him down. "It's okay. Rest. You have work tomorrow, but come right home, because I have a surprise for you. Karen is going to have a movie night with popcorn and pizza for the kids. The two of us will have an evening to ourselves, and it will be only us. I promise. You can make it up to me then."

Matthew snugged down, the rain-cooled air giving the room a fresh scent that soothed him right back to sleep, and he didn't wake until his alarm beeped.

He got up, dressed, and cleaned up quietly before leaving the house and heading to work. He was halfway to town before his mind kicked in and he realized what Lucas had said. Part of him wondered if he had dreamed it, but no, he hadn't. Now that he thought about it, he could remember the words. *It's what you do for the people you love.* Lucas loved him, and just as importantly, he'd not only found a way to say that he loved Matthew, but the entire family. Lucas loved them all, and that warmed Matthew even as the air conditioning worked to cool the interior of his van.

At the plant, he had a mountain of tasks and got right to it. He had a list of repairs and maintenance checks to make. The season hadn't started yet, but in a week or two the lines would be filled with people canning beans and other vegetables that would be brought in by the truckload from as far away as Kentucky. Matthew was one of the year-round employees charged with keeping the facility clean and the equipment in perfect shape, ready for use and inspection. It was a job he took pride in.

"Looking good," the plant manager, John Keller, said as he checked over the canner that heated and sealed the containers.

"Thanks." Matthew closed and locked the electrical access hatch. "I've had to replace the connectors in all these. They were wearing, and I didn't like how they looked."

"Good." John stood, looking out down the production line.

Matthew stood next to his boss. "What's bothering you?" He could always tell. John had hired him seven years earlier, and they had worked together closely.

"Just a feeling, but I can't get it out of my mind that this will be the last year. Nothing has been said…."

"But it's what they aren't saying?" Matthew finished, and John nodded.

"Exactly, but keep this under your hat. Ain't told no one else, and I could be wrong. But there are people who have worked at this place for decades." He sighed. "Don't know when something will be said."

Matthew set his tools in his box. "There have been rumors going through town for the last few years." They were hard to keep ignoring. The plant was aging, and the parent company had been sold a few years ago, so it made sense for them to consolidate. Matthew had always hoped that the folks in town and how hard everyone worked would mean something, but he knew better.

John nodded. "This conversation didn't happen, but if I were you, I'd be looking to see what's available out there. Keep your options open." He put his hands behind his back and continued his walk down the line.

Matthew went back to work, trying to put that out of his mind. He'd deal with things when they happened. With the kids and the way his life was, he could only work through issues as they came up. Trying to head them off took more energy than he could manage. But he'd do what John said and keep his ear to the ground for work.

"What did John want?" Denny asked almost as soon as John was out of sight.

"Just checking to see that we're going to be ready." Denny was a gossip of epic proportions. If you wanted something to get to every corner of the town, all you had to do was tell him. He loved to be in the know. "I know you got stuff to do."

Denny turned and hurried away in the opposite direction from John. Matthew picked up his tools and continued his work. Regardless of the long-term plans for the plant, he had to make sure the equipment was ready for the coming production season, and that meant he needed to get a move on.

He was busy the rest of the afternoon and left the plant on time, pleased with what he'd gotten done. Matthew drove back past the house and stopped in to get a few things and to make sure everything was okay. There was no one hanging around, and he got what he needed before leaving and heading to the lake house.

"Where are the kids?" Matthew asked when Lucas met him in the driveway.

"Inside. Go get changed into jeans and heavy shoes, and then meet me out here once you've seen the kids." He pulled Matthew into a deep kiss. "Karen is watching them, and you're mine for a few hours, like I promised."

"Okay. I'll be back out," Matthew agreed and hurried inside. The kids all said hello and showed him their drawings and the things they'd made with Karen. "I heard you are going to have a movie night."

Brianna bounced on her toes. "Yes. Are you gonna watch with us?"

"I'm going out with Lucas for a while. But you're gonna have popcorn and pizza with Miss Karen, and I'll be home in time to tuck you all in. Okay?"

Brianna nodded, and Matthew talked to each of the kids before they wandered off into the living room.

"Don't worry. Everything is going to be fine." Karen was already getting things set up.

Matthew went to the bedroom and got dressed the way he'd been instructed. Then, after hugging each of the kids goodbye, he found Lucas in the drive and got into the SUV. "Where are we going?"

"To the farm," Lucas said. "I called Geoff and Eli. They have a couple horses saddled up and ready for us."

Matthew grinned. "We're going for a ride?" They hadn't done this since high school. Matthew had been riding a few times over the years, mostly at Geoff's, so he knew the area fairly well. "That's cool. How long has it been for you?"

"I spent quite a bit of time in the saddle for a film I did a few years ago, so I got pretty good, but I haven't been on a horse since. I figured we're just going on a trail ride rather than trying to make our way across the entire west, so we'll be all right."

Matthew shook his head at Lucas's smirk. "Okay." For the drive, he shifted closer to Lucas and held his hand.

They arrived just as Rachel pulled into the farmyard and up to the barn. Geoff and Eli came out to wait for them, Geoff's arm around Eli's waist.

"Everything is ready," Geoff said as they came forward, and everyone shook hands. "Eli is going to make sure you're all set." He smiled before jogging over to the house.

"Come on inside," Eli said. "I wasn't sure how comfortable you were going to be out on your own. I saddled Layla and Thunder for you. Don't let the name fool you—Thunder is as gentle as they come, and he knows the way to the creek. It's one of his favorite trails, so once he knows that's where you're going, you can just relax." He got out a gorgeous bay and helped Lucas into the saddle.

Then Eli brought out Layla, and Matthew mounted. He was familiar with her. "She's an old friend."

"Go on around the barn and then out toward the creek. I put a few things in her saddlebags for you." Eli waved and stepped out of the way. "Have fun and don't worry about anything."

Thunder led the way, and sure enough, he seemed to know where he was going. Layla went behind, the two of them crossing the grassy field. "This is so wonderful," Lucas said.

"It is," Matthew agreed as the wind ruffled his hair, the air fresh and clean.

"It even smells good, without a hint of exhaust or the scent of the city that I never knew was there until I didn't smell it any longer." Lucas's shoulders seemed to lose some of their tension, and he quickly settled into the saddle, moving with the horse. Matthew had learned long ago that the horse needed to be the one to dictate the pace and the feel of the ride. Moving with her was just as easy as watching Lucas in the saddle, that amazing backside rocking with each of Thunder's movements.

For a moment, Matthew let himself dream that they were far away in both distance and time. They could be anywhere or in any era. For now it was just them. "Did you ever think of doing a western?"

Lucas chuckled. "I have a deal for one waiting for me. I have to read the script when I get back. Why?"

Matthew caught up to Lucas. "Because I think you look good on a horse, and maybe it's time the western made a comeback. Especially a sexy one."

"What's a sexy western?"

Matthew rolled his eyes even though Lucas wasn't watching. "One where you spend a good deal of the time with your shirt off, chopping wood, or maybe riding a horse to chase the bad guys half-naked."

Lucas laughed louder. "Okay. So I should specify that there be scenes where I don't wear a shirt."

"Of course. I'd pay for that." He caught up to Lucas. "You'd be sexy half-naked on a horse."

"You just want me to be half-naked now." They reached the edge of the field, still under the canopy of the tall, sprawling trees. Thunder slowed, and they continued until they reached the creek. Then Thunder turned north and continued along the water until they reached a clearing.

"Nope, I want you all naked, but that's probably a bad idea out here." He flashed Lucas a grin and got one in return, along with a nod.

"Wow, I never knew this was here." Lucas dismounted and turned in every direction.

"Not many people do." Matthew dismounted, and the horses made their way to the best grass and began to eat. "Geoff told me once that this was where he and Eli spent part of their time… courting." He couldn't help smiling.

"You're kidding."

"Nope. Eli was the one doing the courting, by the way. He grew up Amish and had a difficult time reconciling his feelings, but he told me that when he did, he decided to court Geoff. He baked him his favorite bread, and they went out riding together. It was his variation on how things would be done back home. He didn't know any other way."

"And it clearly worked, because I have never seen two people more in love." Lucas opened the saddlebag and spread a thin blanket on the ground. Then he pulled out a few containers before sitting. "When I told Geoff I wanted to do this, he said he'd ask Eli to put together a light snack."

Matthew sat and opened a small wax paper bundle. Inside were two slices of homemade cinnamon raisin bread. "Do you think he's trying to tell us something?"

"Maybe." Lucas took the offered slice and nibbled on it before taking a bite. "This is amazing."

"Geoff calls it Eli's love bread," Matthew explained. "He claims it's got magic." He leaned forward, and Lucas met him across the blanket. The kiss started gentle but soon deepened, threatening to take Matthew's breath away. Not that he minded in the least. Lucas pressed him back onto the blanket, and Matthew held him tightly, wrapping his legs around Lucas as their kiss clouded his mind.

In a matter of seconds, nothing else mattered but him and Lucas. "You know I've loved you always. I loved you back in high school." Lucas's gaze met his, hard, heated, and yet soft at the same time. "Being with you again only rekindled what was always there."

"I know," Matthew said softly. "And know that it will always be there." He slipped his hands under Lucas's shirt, hot skin sliding under his palms, making deep impressions on his memory. "I know you have to go back soon, but that isn't going to change how I feel."

Lucas stilled. "It has to." Matthew's mind spun. "You can't put your life on hold. You deserve to be happy and to have someone to share your life. You should be loved, and not just by someone three thousand miles away. I see it all the damned time, relationships that fall apart because of time and distance. I don't want that to happen to us."

Matthew swallowed hard. "Then don't let it." He drew Lucas down to him, their kisses growing more frantic. He realized the energy was coming from him. Lucas was going to have to go, and Matthew was going to stay with the kids while part of his heart got on a plane heading west. There was nothing he could do about it other than impress everything he could onto his memories: the way Lucas kissed him, how his heated skin felt under his hands, the way Lucas's eyes caught the light, glinting when they looked at him.

"But how…?" Lucas whispered.

Matthew didn't have the answer, so instead of saying anything more, he simply tugged at Lucas's shirt, his hands shaking in his near frantic need for contact.

Lucas pulled Matthew up and got his shirt off before they tumbled back down on the blanket, chest to chest, lips to lips, hands roaming in the most delicious way, driving Matthew out of his mind.

The horses neighed, and Lucas stilled as Thunder stomped. Matthew listened past the breeze and the rustle of the grass. Layla neighed, and he turned. Both horses had their noses pointed toward the wind, ears cocked. "Something is going on," Matthew whispered. "Stay here and out of sight." He pulled on his shirt and went over to the horses, stroking Thunder's neck as he peered out through the trees.

Movement caught his eye, and Matthew pulled out his phone and sent a text to Geoff that someone was prowling in the field. After soothing the horses, he made his way to the edge of the trees, where a man with a camera around his neck stood maybe twenty feet away, heading toward the woods. "What do you think you're doing?" Matthew demanded. "This is private property, and you aren't allowed to be here."

"I don't have to answer to you. I'm with the press," he said.

"Really? Trespassing is still illegal, and I can call the police. You can take it up with them." A horse and rider barreled across the field in their direction. "It seems you can take things up with the owner." He shook his head. "I wouldn't want to be you." The guy flinched, and Matthew loved that he paled. It was a good sign.

"Hey, I don't want any trouble. I saw a big SUV pull in and then some guys riding out." He was shaking now, especially with Geoff on his horse charging right toward him. "Jesus Christ!" the guy called out, and Matthew wondered if he was going to wet himself.

"What the hell are you doing on my land?" Geoff demanded as he charged up to the reporter.

"I saw the big SUV, and I heard that Lucas Reardon was still in town," he stammered. "Though the decoy was pretty good and fooled a lot of people."

Geoff drew closer. "And you thought you'd, what… traipse out here, trespass on my land, in the hopes that it was him?" Geoff shook his head.

"That is Lucas Reardon's boyfriend, so I figure I'm on the right track." He straightened his shoulders. "I'll go back to the road and get off your land, but you can't stop me watching the place. If he is here, I'll get my picture and make a bunch of money."

"Actually, I can," Geoff said. "I already called the sheriff. He and I went to school together. He'll take you in and process you for trespassing. That ought to put your spy mission out of commission for a while." Geoff turned to Matthew. "Go on back to your ride. I'll take care of this guy here. He isn't going to bother anyone now." Geoff grinned as a few sheriff's vehicles pulled up to the edge of the field on Stiles Road.

Geoff stayed with his horse as the sheriff marched across the grasses that would eventually be cut for hay.

Matthew walked back under the trees and found Lucas standing with the horses.

"I'm sorry," Lucas said softly, eyes cast down, shirt back on. "I honestly thought you and I could have a little time to ourselves."

"And we can," Matthew said. He walked right up to him and tugged him into a hug. "But I'm starting to feel like the entire world is cockblocking us." He rested his head on Lucas's broad shoulders. "First the kids last night…."

"And then some Jimmy Olsen wannabe today," Lucas added softly as his arms closed around Matthew. "It's all right."

"We could go back to what we were doing," Matthew whispered.

"I don't know if that's a good idea. The last thing I want is pictures of my bare ass in the tabloids… or worse, stories about us."

Matthew tensed. "Are you ashamed?"

Lucas chuckled. "Of you... us? Not in the least. I don't want pictures of you all over the news because you deserve your privacy, and if that happens, you'll get none, and that little fiasco a few days ago on your front lawn will be just the beginning." He pulled away. "Where does that trail go?"

"Along the creek to the east before it turns back toward the farm. It comes out closer to the house, and then we can go around to the barn." Matthew mounted his horse, and Lucas did the same. This time Matthew took the lead, with Lucas close by.

"I figured this would be a good way to get some time alone, and I'm sorry. Maybe it wasn't such a good idea."

Matthew pulled his horse to a stop, and Lucas did the same. Then he reached across and took his hand. "It was a great idea. How could you know that some reporter was going to think that the SUV was connected to you? In fact, he still doesn't. All he got for his troubles was a free ride to the police station, and he'll have to explain what he did to his boss."

"But...." Lucas still seemed upset.

"It was a wonderful idea, and you and I still get to spend time together. And when we get back and the kids are in bed, I'm going to lock the door, and you and I are going to make up for lost time."

Matthew released Lucas's hand and they started forward at a walk next to the gurgling creek. The sun would be setting soon, but the breeze was still fresh.

"I heard something today from Rachel...," Lucas started once they turned away from the creek. "But I don't know how reliable it is or if you want to hear it." He bit his lower lip, a sure sign that Lucas thought he was delivering bad news.

"Is it about the plant?" Matthew asked, his conversation with John fresh in his mind.

"You already know," Lucas said.

"There have been rumors running through town for a while, and the plant is still open." He was hoping that everyone was worried about nothing; it had happened before. When the company was bought out, there were rumors that the plant would be shut down, but it hadn't been. Still.... He pulled Layla to a stop. "You might as well tell me."

"Rachel has her ears to the ground about a lot of things. The parent company is planning to relocate the equipment to another plant in Iowa and close this one down. They'll probably sell the building if they can, but that will be it." He seemed so calm and cool about it, but Matthew wanted to scream his frustration. "But you already know about this."

"I had an idea, yes." He clenched his teeth and balled his hands to fists. "It's the usual story, right? A small town loses its major business and then everyone wonders what will happen next. I'm an electrician and I can find work, I know that, but...."

Lucas nodded, his expression dark. "But everyone else is just going to be out of luck."

"Pretty much. It feels like part of the town is dying." Now it was Lucas's turn to take his hand. "And I wish I could do something. But I'm not an entrepreneur or anything."

Lucas nodded.

"Can I ask how Rachel knows this? The people here are fearful, but no one knows for sure... not even my boss."

"I don't know, but Rachel has sources of information that would make most CEOs jealous." Lucas released his hand and started the horse forward as the sun set behind the trees and shadows fell across the land ahead of them.

"Geoff told me about your interruption," Eli said once they reached the barn. The lights had come on, and Matthew dismounted. Eli led Layla into the barn, and he helped Lucas down before taking Thunder inside as well. "Did you have a good ride anyway?"

"We did, and thank you for the goodies. That was really nice of you." Matthew unsaddled Thunder, then put the tack away. "I don't know what I'm going to do," he added once he realized Lucas wasn't coming inside.

"About Lucas?" Eli asked over the wall from the next stall.

"Yeah. He's going to go back to Hollywood because that's where his work is." Matthew brushed Thunder to get any dust out of his coat. "But I don't want him to leave. And then he's doing this thing on Friday."

"I heard about that on the radio."

Matthew paused and peered over the wall. "He's doing it to raise money and because he and Rachel are hoping to draw out this stalker who won't leave him alone. We have a picture of him, we think, and we're hoping to finally catch the guy. It scares me half to death." He peered down as Eli gently stroked Layla's neck. "I don't know what to do about any of it."

Eli paused and set the brush on one of the boards. "It's pretty simple, as I see it. You go with him and you make sure Lucas is safe, no matter what, because that's what you do for the people you love. Right?"

Matthew nodded. "But the rest?"

"It's not rocket science. You tell Lucas how you feel and what you want. Do you want to go with him? Do you want Lucas to stay? Does it even matter as long as the two of you are together? I left Geoff early on because of some crap with his witch of an aunt and because I wasn't sure I was ready to leave behind the only world I'd ever known. But I was miserable. The community I'd grown up in had gotten too small, and it was missing the one thing I needed most in the world—Geoff."

"How did you figure it out?"

"That was simple. I was honest with myself about what I wanted, and then I went to Geoff and told him. It turned out that he wanted exactly what I did. He wanted me as much as I did him, and we've had more than twenty years together. He and I raised Jakey together, beat cancer together, built this business and a place that's safe for other people like us. And we did it together." He paused. "And who knows what's ahead? There will be good times, and some not so good, but whatever they are, it will be something to two of us face as one. I know that, and there's no better feeling in the world."

"I understand. Having Lucas back has been…." He didn't have the words for it.

"Like finding the other half of yourself that you didn't know was missing?" Eli supplied, and Matthew nodded.

"Exactly. But do I have the right to take the kids away from everything and everyone they know here and move them across the country? Or, almost as bad, how can I ask Lucas to move back here? Either way, it's a lot, and what if things don't work out? What if it's a huge mistake?"

"And what if the two of you are as happy as Geoff and me?" Eli asked and then picked up the brush and returned to taking care of Layla.

Matthew backed away from the wall and wished he had some sort of answer to rebut Eli, but it was hard to argue with a possibility that he had always hoped would turn out to be true. Damn it all, some people just got the best lines… and he wished it was him.

CHAPTER 11

"YOU LOOK silly," Carl said with a giggle as Rachel worked on her tablet, dressed as an early Michigan settler in rough old-time clothes. Lucas had to admit that the kid had a point.

"Thanks, Carl," she said with a grin, then made a face that made all the kids laugh.

"Why can't we go too?" Brianna asked.

Will groaned. "Because they're doing grown-up stuff tonight and we're going to stay here with Miss Karen. She's making pizza, and Uncle Lucas got us a Nintendo, so we're going to play video games."

Matthew hadn't been thrilled with the gift, but Lucas had told him that the kids were staying home because of him, so he wanted them to have something special. Rachel had hooked up the game to the big television in the living room, so they were going to have Mario Kart races in surround sound. Lucas might have to give Karen hazard pay.

Lucas was already dressed, and he went up to check on Matthew, who was still trying to pick out a shirt.

"What do you wear to an event designed to catch a stalker? Plaid, earth tones, a bloodred shirt?" He nervously paced the room. "I don't like this at all."

"I don't either, but we need to put this guy out of commission. He's reported where I am, where we are, and scared the kids. Last time he broke into my trailer on the studio, and we believe he tried to get into my house. That guy on Geoff's land was there because of the trouble Ruetoyou has stirred up." He sat on the edge of the bed. "We need to get this guy, if for no other reason than to find out why he's so damned obsessed. I keep dreaming that I'm being chased, sometimes through the woods, the last time through the grocery store, but I can never see the guy. I woke up all sweaty and scared last night."

Matthew put his head on Lucas's shoulder, and Lucas wanted nothing more than the rip his stalker apart. Coming after him was one thing, but Matthew and his family were quite another. Lucas had signed up for this shit, in a way—he was a public figure. But Matthew and the kids certainly hadn't.

"Then let's try to get this guy so we can stop those dreams of yours and have some quiet time together." Matthew didn't say anything about leaving, but it was on the horizon. They both knew it, but it was something neither of them brought up. There had been times when Lucas thought that Matthew might want be open to talking about it, like last night once the kids were in bed and Matthew had locked the door. But then Matthew had decided that talking was the last thing he wanted, and they had put their mouths and lips to much better use. Still, it was something Lucas couldn't put off much longer.

"And wear the plaid. It's sexy."

"It makes me look like an emaciated lumberjack."

Lucas bumped his shoulder. "It does not. So wear what you want and let's get ready to go."

Matthew chose a light blue shirt and shrugged it on. "Why aren't you nervous?" he asked when he fumbled the buttons. He huffed, and Lucas gently batted his hands away.

"I'm an actor," he said as calmly as he could while doing up Matthew's buttons, his hand brushing warm, smooth skin. "Just relax. The most important thing is to see and be seen. People will want to talk and say hello. They're paying for the chance to spend a few minutes with me." He smoothed the fabric over Matthew's chest. "I don't mean to sound vain or anything."

"I know, and part of why I'm going is to make sure that you're safe." He took a deep breath and then sighed dramatically. "Let's say goodbye to the kids and go." He paused at the bedroom door. "And for the record, the only reason I'm letting you do this is because I have a dozen friends who are going to be there watching out for us."

Lucas cocked his head to the side. "You're *letting* me do this?"

Matthew flashed him the cockiest expression ever, complete with a glint in his eyes. "Yes. I'm glad you recognized that." He opened the door, chuckling softly.

Lucas rolled his eyes and followed Matthew to where the kids were already making use of the game. They both got hugs and said their goodbyes, with Matthew promising to tuck all of them in when he got home.

"We're going to be late," Rachel said, and after a final round of goodbyes, they left.

Rachel drove them through Ludington and across the river flats before turning right and up into the bluffs that overlooked Lake Michigan.

"I was instructed to park in the employee area," Rachel explained as they turned into a drive past the main entrance. They headed up around the side, where Haven met the car and ushered them all inside.

"We have two other people dressed casually who will mix with the attendees, and they have pictures of the man we're after."

"And there are twelve friends who will be attending. They also have a picture, and they will contact Rachel if they see him," Matthew explained. "Remember that the most important thing is keeping Lucas safe."

"Agreed," Rachel said. "Though getting some answers from this guy will certainly go a long way to doing that." Her eyes were darker than usual, and she definitely seemed more predatory. Rachel was in her element, and she was determined. "All questions will come through me, and I will stay close by. Haven will be more visible. He's the muscle, and I'm going to act as the eyes and ears."

"What do we do if we see him?" Matthew asked.

"Just pretend you have a message. Everyone uses their phones. Then text me where he is. Don't try to take a picture or let on that you've spotted him. We'll take it from there."

"What will you do then?"

"We aren't law enforcement, so we can't arrest him, even though there are charges pending in California. Here it's a different story. We'll try to get information out of him and then call the police, leave it up to them."

"So he hasn't broken any laws," Matthew said.

"Not as far as we know. But we believe he has in California. He's wanted in connection with the break-ins of Lucas's house and trailer. It's thin, I know, but what we really need is information, especially on why he's so fascinated with Lucas in particular."

"Okay," Matthew agreed.

"Good. We're being told that they are opening the front gates for the event, so they want you to get into position near the meeting house. People will meet you, and they will have staff dressed in costume that will keep people moving. I'll be one of them and right nearby."

"Okay." Lucas had done events like this many times. Early on in his career, he'd sat at autograph event tables for hours meeting people and signing pictures. "Matthew will stay next to me."

"Yes. You will have plenty of people nearby. If you feel uncomfortable or threatened, simply tell Matthew that you're hungry and want a banana. That will be our signal to step in." Rachel handed her tablet to Haven, who moved off. A few other people dressed in period costume joined them.

"I'm Lisa, and this is Michelle." They were both in their midforties and seemed intent on their job.

"It's very nice to meet you," Lucas said, shaking hands with both of them. Matthew did the same, and they took up positions nearby. They directed people, made introductions, and kept the line moving. Lucas chatted with everyone, smiling until his cheeks ached. The people he recognized—friends of Matthew's—kept their distance, looking at other exhibits, letting others have their moments.

About half an hour in, Eli joined those in line. "It's good to meet you," Eli said in a normal tone before adding softly, "I think he's at the end of the line. Jeans, lime green shirt, fancy camera."

Lucas's heart sped up as he spoke briefly to Eli. "Tell Rachel. She just stepped inside for a minute." Lucas kept smiling as Eli moved on. He tried not to make a big deal of attempting to see who Eli was referring to.

Fortunately, Matthew had a better view, and he nodded. "It looks like him. What do we do?"

"Nothing," Rachel said. "I have it well in hand." She stood nearby as the line continued. Lucas saw people coming through a second time, and that was fine. He played it up, watching as the man in lime green grew closer.

Matthew stepped back, slightly behind Lucas, when the man was next in line. Lucas was fairly sure he had seen him before, but he kept to his script, greeted him, and thanked him for coming and supporting the historical society, acting as though he weren't familiar.

"It was so good of you to come," Matthew added.

"I had to see Lucas." The way Matthew turned and watched him raised goose bumps on Lucas's arms and made him feel naked at the same time. "I'm a huge fan and never miss an opportunity."

Lucas had to keep any sort of reaction off his face. This was his stalker—Lucas knew it—and he was right there. Still, he had to let him continue on.

Matthew pulled out his phone, but Rachel gently patted each of them on the shoulder. "Would you like some water?" She handed them each a bottle. "I have this," she whispered, and then moved away. "Sir," she called to the man in the lime shirt. "You won the special door prize. You're the hundredth person through the line."

"I am?" he asked. "I did?"

"Yes. Lucas signed some posters from his last movie, and each hundredth person gets one."

The guy was buying her load of crap, and he followed Rachel inside. Lucas *had* signed some posters, but he knew she was just using that as bait. He relaxed slightly and continued talking with the guests, hoping this was finally over.

Rachel returned a few minutes later, shaking her head. Lucas inwardly groaned, but he took a drink of water and finished saying hello to everyone before going inside himself.

"What happened?" he asked once they were alone. The guests were now fanning out through the village and would come together in an hour outside the meeting house, where Lucas was scheduled to do a dramatic reading from *The Scarlet Letter*.

"It wasn't him. I asked to see identification, and it was local and most definitely his. A few minutes later a woman and a girl, who he introduced as his wife and daughter, hurried up all excited."

"Okay. There was no one else that might be him?" Matthew asked.

Rachel shook her head. "Not that I saw, but at least we didn't give ourselves away. There are still a few people coming in. We'll have another chance at the reading. In the meantime...."

"I know. I'm all set." Lucas tried his best to hide his disappointment.

"It was a long shot in the first place, and we were counting on a number of assumptions that may not have happened."

Lucas knew that, but still, he had hoped that they could lure out their man and have this over with. Shaking his head, he returned outside and greeted people as they passed.

"Was this a last-minute event?" a man asked as Lucas shook his hand. He kept looking around, and then gripped Lucas's hand more tightly. "How are you finding your hometown after so many years? It must be a little... strange for you to be back." He smiled, and those eyes bored into him, giving him *Exorcist*-level creeps. "It's a nice town, but I guess it doesn't compare to Hollywood with all the things the city can offer."

"It's been very nice being home again. I've reconnected with my family and said goodbye to my father. I also got to visit with friends again." Lucas decided to keep his answers bland and uninteresting. "Hollywood is big and fast. It has its bright spots, but so does being back here, with its slower pace and the chance to get to know the people I grew up with again." He smiled and turned his attention to the family behind the fan.

The teenager held a book, and Lucas leaned forward to engage her. "I loved you as Superboy, and I didn't believe Daddy when he told me you grew up here." She put her hand to her mouth like she was sharing a secret. "He kids a lot."

"Just one more question," the pushy man said.

"I'm sorry," Matthew said, already guiding him away. "Lucas has other people he needs to speak with. But I can talk to you, if you like. Lucas and I have been friends for a long time." Matthew's voice trailed off as he led the man inside, and Lucas could just imagine Rachel pouncing on him in her settler's garb.

Matthew returned a few moments later as Haven and some of the others that Lucas assumed were part of his security hurried inside.

"What's all that?" the father asked.

"Nothing to worry about. We aren't going to let people be rude." He smiled. "Would you like me to sign your book for you?" The girl bounced on her feet and shoved it toward him. "What's your name?"

"Violet," she answered. Lucas wrote an inscription to her, signed beneath it, and then posed for pictures with her and her family. They thanked him and moved on through the village.

"We got him," Matthew said, and Lucas went on to greet the remaining people. Then he excused himself and went inside and to the front of the room, where Rachel and Haven stood with the man from earlier.

"There's no law against asking questions."

Rachel stepped forward. "That's true, but when you came in here, I was able to pull a print from where you touched that chair, and it matches one we found inside Lucas's trailer in California." She was laying her bluff on thick. "This is a long way to come for a simple story about anyone, even Lucas Reardon."

"You can't hold me," he said, squaring his shoulders. "You aren't the police."

"No, we aren't," Lucas told him. "But I pressed charges, and we can call the police and make sure we let them know that you're wanted out there. They'll cuff you and stick you in a cell to wait for extradition."

"Exactly," Rachel added. "That could take weeks or longer. After all, there's no real hurry on anyone's part. And they don't allow bail for people waiting on extradition. You simply sit in jail." That got to him. "So my question is… are you going to cooperate or not, Anthony Tedesco? We know who you are and where you live, and from there we can find out anything we need to about you." Rachel's eyes were hard as steel with a hint of fire fresh from the furnace.

"Lucas, you're expected at the reading in a few minutes, and people are going to be coming in."

Rachel nodded. "So are you going to play ball, or do we wait here for the police and let them deal with you? By the way, that doesn't mean you'll be done with us, just locked up."

Anthony shivered. "Who the hell are you, anyway?" His shoulders slumped, and Rachel's lips quirked upward for a few seconds. Then she schooled her expression.

"They're my security," Lucas growled.

Anthony looked from face to face, probably for support, and then back at Rachel. "What do you want to know?"

Rachel nodded, and Haven got Anthony out of the chair. Then he and Rachel ushered him out the back door as people began flowing into the space set up for the reading.

THE PROGRAM was a success. Lucas had done this sort of thing before and knew how to build up the drama. He didn't read the entire novel, of course, but he did read some of the best parts, as well as speak some about the life early settlers led. Then he opened the floor to questions and ended up explaining what he could about his upcoming projects.

"Thank you so much for coming," Lucas said at the end of the program. "I hope you had as wonderful a time as I did." He waved to applause and then stepped off the dais, where Matthew met him with Rachel, and they ushered him to the car.

"What did you find out?" Lucas asked as soon as the door was closed and they were on their way back.

"The guy is a real piece of work. Anthony is the guy who stalked you last year. We apparently got close enough to him then that he gave up and moved on to someone else." Rachel headed back out toward the freeway. "That's why things were quiet for so long."

"Then why did he follow me here and pick things up again?" Lucas asked. "It's a long way to come."

Rachel slowed for a light and pulled to a stop. "That's the strange thing. He said he was contacted through his social media and told where you would be and that it wasn't likely any other of the Hollywood press would be here. They said he could have near exclusive access if he wanted it. So Anthony jumped on a plane and arrived a day after you did. He said it wasn't too hard to find you, especially with the funeral, and all he did was follow you out to the state park."

"Okay, I guess that makes sense, but what about the rest of it? Why would he put out the word on the hotel and Matthew's place? It doesn't make sense if what he wanted was exclusive pictures. Keeping a low profile would benefit him, not being a pain in the ass like that."

Rachel grew quiet for a few minutes, and Lucas began to wonder what was going on. "The thing is… someone was telling him what to do, feeding him information and getting some from him. Anthony only knows a name on social media, but he was sent funds so he could go on the trip, and he says he got more money each time he reported where you were."

"What the hell?" Lucas asked as he sat back in the seat. "None of this makes sense. Who would want to broadcast my location to the rest of the world? What sort of reward is there in it for anyone? Guys like Anthony make their money getting exclusive pictures. They don't advertise their targets, nor do they shout it to the rest of the world when they get inside information." He took Matthew's hand, agitated beyond belief. He had hoped to get some answers once they caught this damned stalker, but all he had was more questions, and none of it made any sense. His head ached. He just wanted to go back to the house and hide for a while. Never before had he been so damned tempted to grab a bottle of Scotch and drink himself into oblivion.

"Okay, wait," Matthew said. "First thing, where is Anthony now? What have you done with him?" The amusement in Matthew's voice told Lucas he was imagining all kinds of nasty things.

"We couldn't hold him, and he was forthcoming with what he knew," Rachel explained.

"And you believed him?" Matthew asked. She nodded as she drove. "But where is he?"

"Right now he's with Haven at the hotel we're using."

Lucas sighed and closed his eyes, fatigue catching up with him.

"Take us there." He was so forceful. "I have a few questions I want to ask this guy." The banked fury in Matthew's tone sent a shock of energy up Lucas's spine. "And before you ask, yes, I'm sure. This man has caused a great deal of trouble."

Rachel slowed and got off the freeway, heading into Ludington to one of the small hotels out by the lake. She parked, and Matthew squeezed Lucas's hand. "I'm coming with you." Lucas had his own questions. Still, he wasn't sure how many answers they were going to get, but he did want to ask his questions.

Rachel led them around the side of the building. She knocked and then unlocked a hotel room door. Anthony lay on the bed, a bottle of beer on the table beside him, a bag of Doritos on his belly. Haven sat at the table with a laptop, typing away.

"What are you doing here?" Anthony asked, sitting up as Lucas glared at him.

"I wanted to talk to you," Lucas told him flatly.

"I already told your hired help everything I know. They're taking me to the airport tomorrow, and I'll be out of your hair. But there will be others who follow me. There always are." He made it sound like they were a pack of rabid dogs, and maybe that was a good description.

"You said you don't know who paid you," Matthew said. "How did you know you would be paid? And are you in the habit of taking orders from unnamed people? You didn't know who this guy was, but you followed instructions like some robot."

"I get paid lots of ways, and as long as they pay, I do what I have to." His bravado seemed to wither under Matthew's intensity. Frankly, it was sexy as hell the way Matthew went all bulldog for Lucas. "It's part of this business. We get paid for the pictures we take and nothing more. So when a guy like me gets good information, we try to keep the gravy train running." Anthony took a swig of his beer and then set the bottle down again.

Lucas sat on the side of the bed, hoping whatever darkness made this guy do what he did didn't rub off on him. Lucas sat there quietly, watching this weasel of a man, when something that had been niggling the back of his mind came into focus. "You said that you stopped pursuing me last year because you thought we were getting too close to you." He found that strange, because as far as he knew, they hadn't gotten that close at all.

"Yeah, what of it? I thought I did a good job of covering my tracks. All I thought anybody had on me was some dumb screen name." Anthony leaned forward. "But then I got a message at home to back off or else. That scared me, so I did as they asked. Getting threats online is no big deal, but they knew where I lived."

"Who sent you the message?" Lucas asked.

Anthony shrugged and then leaned forward again, his eyes becoming more animated. "I didn't know at first. But I'm pretty good at finding shit out. The top of the page had been cut off, and I didn't know why until I figured out they used paper from their office and cut off the letterhead. From there and from what a neighbor told me, I thought it was from your manager's office."

"Leon Sanders?" Lucas asked. "You think he was onto you?"

Anthony shrugged. "Yeah. So I backed off." He smiled a little weakly. "I always liked your movies. That was why I started following you in the first place. I was a fan, and I got some really good pictures. I guess I let things get out of hand. Sometimes I get caught up in shit and I don't know when to stop. But when I saw that note at home, I knew I had gone too far." He finished his beer and leaned back against the headboard.

"What's so special about Lucas?" Matthew asked, and Lucas felt himself scowl. "I didn't mean it that way, and you know it," Matthew added quietly, placing his hands on Lucas's aching shoulders.

"He was always a nice guy, even when we were trying to get pictures of him. He would smile and wave sometimes, like he thought of us as people. I actually came to like you," Anthony added. "I think that was why I get it in my head that… well… I got obsessed in a way. I used to follow you all over the city all the time. But then you got security, and this note shows up, and I knew I'd gone too far, so I left you to other people."

Matthew gently massaged Lucas's muscles. "Do you think your agent got involved?"

Lucas's mind ran in circles, and he needed a chance to think a minute. "Leon knew who you were and how to find you."

Rachel nodded and scowled.

Lucas shrugged and stood. "Thank you for answering our questions. One of the security people will take you back to Grand Rapids and put you on a plane home. From there, what you do is up to you. I'll make sure that the complaint against you is dropped."

"Do you think that's a good idea?" Rachel asked.

Lucas kept his gaze on Anthony. "I do. Because now this man owes me a favor. I could send him to jail, but he cooperated, and I know he isn't going to cause any trouble for us any longer. Isn't that right?" He waited until Anthony nodded. "Good. Make sure he gets on the plane and makes it home." Lucas stood and left the room, then returned to the SUV. He waited in the back seat for Matthew, hugging him as soon as he got inside.

"I take it your agent never mentioned anything about knowing who your stalker was," Matthew said. Lucas shook his head. "What do you think he was trying get away with?"

Lucas sighed. "I don't know. The last time I talked to him, he was asking me where I was. I gave him evasive answers, but now I'm wondering if there wasn't something more to it than I thought. I was just after a little privacy. I didn't think...." That was the problem.

"What are you going to do?" Matthew swallowed hard, his eyes filling with worry.

"It seems I'm going to have to have a heart-to-heart with Leon, and I'm probably going to need to do it sooner rather than later."

Matthew nodded slowly. "So when are you going to leave?" He sat back in the seat and said nothing more, but his shoulders slumped. "I know you have to go, but...."

Lucas took a deep breath and glanced at the back of Rachel's head, wishing they had privacy for this conversation. Even though he knew Rachel would say nothing and would immediately forget anything that was said in the car, it seemed wrong, and yet there were things he had to say. "I would love nothing more than for you and the kids to come out to LA. I could sell my house, and we could get one together that would be big enough for the kids to have their own rooms. I'd... I don't know. Make room for all of you. The kids could go to the best schools, and they would have all the opportunities possible. They would have everything the city has to offer."

"Yeah?" Matthew asked. "And what about you? Would we have you in our lives, or would you be gone for months at a time? Losing Eden made me realize that all the money in the world isn't going to fill my life with love, and that it's the people that are really important." He took Lucas's hand, squeezing it. "I know that you would do your best to make room for us. I have no doubt. But...." He hesitated and seemed to search for the words. "The temptation would be too much. I know you love what you do, and I worry that you'd resent us. You've been with the kids for a week or so, but there's no going back for me. I'll be raising the children for the next twenty years in one form or another. Are you really up for that?" He squeezed his hand, and Lucas wondered if Matthew thought so little of him. "And just so you know, I'm not being mean, and I don't think you wouldn't be a good dad, because you would. There are days that I wonder if I'm up for it, but it's a lot to take on, and there's no going back. Those kids already adore you, but they know you're leaving."

Lucas leaned close enough to fill his nose with Matthew's scent. "I didn't make the offer lightly. And it's a lot to ask. The kids would be taken away from everything they know, and they'd be starting over. But I want you to know that the offer stands. I want you and the kids to be my family, and if that means now, or later… I know it's what I want. I could see us taking the kids to Disneyland and Catalina Island. We'd visit all the national parks and see Europe… as a family."

"I know, and I want that too. But you said yourself you work all the time. When would we be able to do that?" Matthew asked.

Lucas pictured his schedule for the next year, and he lowered his head, knowing Matthew was right.

"It's not that I don't want to be with you. I've dreamed of it for years, but I can't expect you to change your life any more than you can expect for the kids and me to pick up everything and move. It's too big a step right now." Matthew hugged him hard. "But I love you for making the offer." Matthew kissed him gently as they pulled into the community and then up to the house.

Lucas had put his cards on the table, and while he'd known it was a long shot, he had played what he had. But the kids trumped everything… and they had to.

Chapter 12

"Thank you for everything," Matthew told Karen once the kids had all been read to and were finally settled in bed. He popped open a bottle of white wine and poured glasses for those who wanted some. "The kids are now calling you Aunt Karen."

She seemed tickled, judging by her smile. "I hope it's okay. They asked if they could call me that."

"I think it's fine." He sat on the sofa, and Lucas joined him, taking a glass. Karen took her glass and ensconced herself at the snack bar with her tablet.

"You need to give yourself the evening off," Lucas told her. "I hope you're doing what you want instead of running down emails or checking my messages."

"I am. Everything is caught up as far as I know, and there haven't been any burning fires in the past few days. Though I do understand that you had a successful evening. No more stalker?"

Lucas turned, looking over the back of the sofa. "Yeah. Just some weird twists and turns. Someone was feeding him information and money. They paid for him to come here, and we don't know why. It's unnerving."

Karen rolled her eyes dramatically. "Leon?"

Matthew nearly dropped his glass. Lucas managed to set his on the table without dumping it down his front or doing a spit take. "Why do you say that?"

"It's pretty obvious. He hates the very idea of you being out of town. He keeps sending me messages asking where you are and if you're okay. He seems to think that I'm your babysitter and that I work for him." She shook her head. "The guy is a real douche. He's nice to you, but he's a shit to everyone else."

"How so?" Matthew asked when Lucas started coughing. He patted his back and then rubbed it, letting Lucas catch his breath.

"No one really notices us around the set and stuff. Stars and big-time agents act like we're part of the fixtures, like the toilets or something. But we talk. They all avoid Leon, and there are stories of actors dumping him because he wanted to control everything about them. The guy sounded creepy to me." She went back to her tablet, and Lucas sat on the sofa once more.

"Jesus," he breathed.

"It's okay. You can't know everything about everyone."

"No. But how did I miss that? He always shows up when I'm on location, and when I'm filming in the studio, it seems like he's...."

"Hovering?" Karen asked. "That's because he is. No one else's agent does that."

"And I thought it was because I was important to him."

Karen scoffed. "You are. But he's a control freak. And I'd guess he's going crazy because you're away from him and he can't influence you." She grabbed her tablet and came to where Lucas sat. "I'm sorry if I spoke out of turn."

Lucas seemed stunned and was deep in thought. "You didn't," Matthew assured her. "You said what you did because you care."

"How could I have missed that?" Lucas asked again, and Matthew figured it was to no one in particular.

"There's nothing you can do about it right now." Matthew tried to comfort Lucas, but he wound tighter by the second. "Try to relax and not think about it for a while." Even as he offered the advice, he knew it would be impossible. Matthew wouldn't be able to put it aside either.

Karen said good night and quietly left the room. Rachel had already left to go on one of her evening walk-arounds of the property. Matthew turned out the lights, letting the darkness from outside slip in. "I know this is another reason why you have to go sooner rather than later."

"I know. Maybe you and the kids could come out to California," Lucas offered. Matthew found himself nodding, but he knew it wasn't practical. "You see right through me, don't you?"

"I always did," Matthew told him. "If we come out, when would you have time? Six months, a year?" He sighed. "We keep coming back to this. What we've had is wonderful, but it's a summer thing. You were on vacation and could spend all the time in the world with us. But that's ending, and you need to go back to your life... and I need to do the same. We'll move home first thing Monday morning. I have to go to work, and

I have the kids registered for day camp through the school." He shrugged to try to cover, but Matthew knew it was going to rip him apart to say goodbye to Lucas again.

Lucas finished his wine and then stood, taking Matthew's hand. Matthew got up and left the glasses on the table, letting Lucas lead him to the bedroom.

Matthew had always known they would come to this, but he wouldn't trade his time with Lucas for anything. Lucas closed their bedroom door behind them and locked it with a snick. Then he cupped Matthew's cheek, kissing him deeply, driving Matthew wild as he pressed him back against the mattress.

"Lucas, I…," Matthew whispered, but Lucas shook his head.

"No talking and no words. Not right now. Nothing is going to change today or tomorrow, and we both have to do what we need to. But for now, it's just us." Matthew looked into those eyes that had entranced so many people from the big screen. "Whatever happens isn't going to change the fact that I love you and I always have."

"I love you too," Matthew said, his throat aching as Lucas cut off further conversation, kissing him down onto the bed. "For the record, I don't want you to go. I want to make that clear."

"I know. It's written in your eyes." Lucas's voice grew rough, and he slipped his arms around Matthew's back, holding him tightly without moving. "And just so you know, I want to strip you naked and memorize every inch of you for those times when I'm lying awake in that damned trailer and can't sleep. At least then I'll be able to remember what it was like to have you next to me." Lucas lay still, and Matthew hugged him in return. The passion that had been building seemed to cool, not because Matthew wasn't ready and willing, but it just didn't seem like the moment.

"I want the same thing," Matthew said.

"Then why am I so content just to hold you?" Lucas asked and then sighed.

"Because maybe there are times when there are things more intimate than sex." Matthew shimmied, and Lucas rolled away. Matthew stripped off the last of his clothes and climbed under the covers. Lucas did the same. Then Lucas slid close, slipping an arm around his waist, and Matthew sighed, leaning back into Lucas's spoon, one of his hands making small circles on his belly.

"I...."

Matthew closed his eyes and waited for what Lucas wanted to say.

"Sometimes I just don't understand."

"What?"

"Me, myself, us.... There are times when I think I'm not made right. Most guys would have sex no matter what and to hell with everything else. You know what I mean?"

Matthew nodded slowly. "I do know what you mean. But sex is just one part of a relationship. One of the good parts, surely, but so is being there and supporting each other, putting yourself second to the other... and to their needs." Matthew slowly rolled over. "I knew a couple—we went to high school with them. Do you remember Shirley and Nate?"

"I do. They were the cover picture for *Cute Couple* magazine." They each chuckled at the use of their old catty joke.

"They got married a year after graduation... and fought all the time. Eden told me all about it. She and Shirley stayed friends. Anyway, Shirley reportedly wanted to go to college, while Nate wanted someone to stay home and look after the house. Even though he was working at the gas station out toward Custer and they were living with her folks. The marriage lasted a year... then Shirley left and did what she thought she had to. She graduated from Ferris in business and now works at Intel in plant management. The last time I saw Nate, he was asking me if I wanted fries or apples with Brianna's Happy Meal. They were so good in high school, but when the rubber hit the road, neither of them was willing to compromise or see the other's point of view. Instead, they both tried to impose their will on the other. That isn't a life, that's a life sentence."

"I want you to be happy, and I want to be happy, and right now it seems that both things just aren't possible. Not as things stand."

"No, they don't seem to be. But things can and do change. That's one of the constants of the universe." He rested his head against Lucas's shoulder. "One way or another, we'll figure things out." And if they didn't and the two of them were destined to go their own way, then.... Matthew didn't want to think about that right now.

"I hope you're right," Lucas said softly.

Matthew snickered. "Haven't you figured out by now that I usually am?" He closed his eyes and waited for sleep to overtake him. Thankfully, he didn't have to work in the morning, but the kids would be up early, anxious to watch television or to go down to the lake. Lucas held him a little closer, and that was enough for now. Matthew had to hope that things would work out one way or another.

"DO YOU really have to go?" Carl asked Sunday morning. Matthew joined the rest of the family in the living room. Carl sat on Lucas's lap as they watched Disney Junior together.

"I do. I have to go back so I can make more movies and stuff." He smiled over Carl's head, and Matthew forced one in return. Time seemed to fly faster and faster as the hours passed. "Maybe you and Uncle Daddy can come to visit sometime. If you do, I'll be sure to show you how movies are made."

"Me too?" Gregory asked.

"All of you. I promise." Lucas yawned, and Matthew went to the kitchen for coffee.

"Can we?" Carl asked as though they were going to leave with Lucas. "Please, Uncle Daddy?" He turned on the big eyes and wobbly lower lip.

"Maybe someday." He sipped his coffee and let it work its magic. "But while Lucas is still here, let's go have some fun, okay? We can go swimming and play in the sand."

"And we can go out on the boat," Lucas offered.

"I go get my bathing suit." Carl jumped off Lucas's lap and raced off.

"I'll make sure he puts everything on right," Will offered and followed him out of the room. Matthew couldn't help thinking how quickly Will was growing up.

Matthew sat on the sofa and put his feet up, trying to put on a brave face and not be Mr. Grumpypants. He was not going to obsess over Lucas leaving. After finishing his coffee, Matthew put together a quick breakfast and got the kids seated. He even managed to get Carl to take off his swimmies… for now.

"Eat the last of your apples," Matthew coaxed Brianna. "And you need to finish your toast," he added to Carl. Thankfully the other two finished and went into the living room. Carl shoved the last bite into his mouth before getting down and hurrying into the living area so he could watch too. "Do you want to come to the lake with us?" he asked Karen.

"Thank you, but no. I have a lot of arrangements and appointments to make. I figured I'd get all that done while you're gone and the house is quiet." Not that Matthew could blame her for a second. There were times—at least ten a day—that he wished he could have a quiet house for, like, ten minutes. That was all he needed, ten minutes of pure quiet. Maybe that would happen in twenty years or so. He ate the last of his own food and drank some coffee while Lucas scooped Carl into his arms and zoomed him around like an airplane, to giggles.

"Let's get all of you ready to go swimming and then out on the boat, okay?" Lucas said with more energy than Matthew could possibly manage. All of them hurried to their room, except Carl, whom Lucas zoomed over to him. Then Lucas hurried off, and Matthew sat with his youngest, finishing his coffee.

"Are you sad?" Carl asked.

Matthew nodded. "A little," he lied, but how did he explain to a four-year-old that he was losing the one person who made his heart seem whole? That was more than what Carl could understand. "I'm going to miss Lucas."

Carl leaned against his chest. "Me too." He patted Matthew's arm. "He gives good airplane rides."

Matthew couldn't help chuckling as he wished things were that simple for him as well. Lucas returned, and Carl slipped down to ask for another ride. Matthew used the time he was occupied to put on his own suit and check on his three other hoodlums. He adjusted Brianna's suit and got towels and sun shirts for the boys, a cover-up for Brianna, and snacks for all of them.

By the time they headed out the door and down the stairs to the sand, Matthew felt like a pack rat. He relieved himself of the burden once they were on the boat.

"Everyone sit down, and you need to stay that way," Lucas said while he helped with life jackets. Then Lucas started the engine, and they were off.

Carl immediately came over, and Matthew lifted him onto his lap. Brianna and her older brothers seemed fascinated as they slid across the water. Matthew knew he was luckier than most. He had four healthy, amazing kids, and his life was pretty full. But all it took was a turn of his head to where Lucas stood at the wheel of the boat, the wind blowing his hair, and seeing that smile, for him to know that no matter how full his life was, there was going to be a hole come tomorrow morning.

"THAT WAS an amazing day." Matthew blinked as he listened to the sound of a quiet house. Carl had been asleep for two hours, and the others were out like lights. Nothing like a day on the water and playing on the beach to wear them out. Well, that and then a huge dinner for Geoff, Eli, Matthew's friends, and Lucas's aunt in order to say goodbye. "Thank you for all of it." Karen had apparently made all the arrangements, and Rachel had taken care of the travel.

Lucas had to be up very early for the drive to Grand Rapids, but that didn't show for a second as he slipped under the covers and turned out the light.

"Nothing is going to be the same."

Lucas rolled over and tugged Matthew to him. Matthew slipped closer, his legs sliding between Lucas's as he pressed him onto the mattress. "No, it won't." He held Matthew in his gaze and then closed the distance between them. The kiss left Matthew light-headed, and Lucas deepened it.

"Lucas, I...."

Lucas shook his head. "You're mine tonight. There aren't going to be any interruptions. No kids, no storms—I checked. Karen and Rachel have orders to keep everyone away from this room on pain of death. So tonight, you're mine. For this one night, there's nothing outside this room." Lucas smoothed back the hair that threatened to flop into Matthew's eyes. "It's just you and me, and there's only one rule."

"What's that?"

"You can't make too much noise." Lucas put a finger to his lips and then slid down under the sheet.

Matthew chuckled at the implication, which came to fruition with intense suction that cut off any sound Matthew made and had him arching his back and gripping the bedding as a tsunami of pleasure pounded over him. He had been totally unprepared for that, just as he was for when the happy train came to an abrupt end. He groaned, but Lucas kissed away any sound, holding him in that gaze that mesmerized millions from the big screen. Only this was just for him. It was special. Everyone else could watch this amazing man on their television or in the theater, but only Matthew got him in person.

Minutes and hours passed as they moved together, with Lucas the master of anticipation, until Matthew knew he was going to blow apart into a million pieces. Only then did Lucas push him over the edge, the two of them flying together on wings of passion, only to return to earth holding each other as the cool night air caressed their weary, sweat-soaked bodies.

All Matthew's energy had been spent, and Lucas held him as he closed his eyes. "I do love you," Lucas whispered as he kissed that spot behind his ear. Matthew told Lucas he loved him too as sleep washed over him. He wanted to stop it, to hold on to this moment for as long as possible, but he couldn't. When he woke again, the bed was empty.

Lucas stood next to him, fully dressed. He leaned over the bed to kiss him, and then, almost like a ghost, he was gone. Matthew rolled over, clamped his eyes closed, and tried not to let in the loneliness that already threatened to overwhelm him.

CHAPTER 13

THERE WERE times when he hated to travel, and every single one of the past twelve hours fell into that category. Rachel had traveled with him as far as Chicago. She'd made sure he got on his flight and hadn't been bothered before taking her own flight on to her next assignment.

"Are you sure I can't entice you to stay on?" Lucas had asked her.

Rachel had paused a few seconds. "Let me think about it. I love what I do, and I get to meet the most amazing people. I promise to give it some thought, though." That was all he could ask.

Lucas settled into his seat, put on headphones and a sleep mask, downed a couple of whiskeys, and went to sleep. He woke hours later when it was time to deplane. Karen ushered him through the terminal with her usual efficiency, and they got his luggage and went right to the car with a minimum of fuss. Traffic was its usual mess, and it took well over an hour to get home.

Lucas took his bag to his room before wandering through the empty house, with its wall of glass overlooking the pool and the city beyond. The house had three bedrooms, an open living and kitchen area, and an office. It wasn't huge, but it felt empty after two weeks with Matthew and the kids.

"Where would you like me to start?" Karen asked.

Lucas shook his head. "What I want you to do is go home and take a rest for a few days. You went above and beyond, and I appreciate it so much. Go out with some friends." He pulled out his wallet and handed her two hundred-dollar bills. "Have some fun." He pressed them into her hand. "I'll be fine for a few days."

"Are you sure?" she asked.

"Yes. Go. And thank you for everything." He gave her a smile, and she left the house, probably before he had a chance to change his mind. Once he was alone, he unpacked and tried to get a sense of being back once more.

Lucas loved his house, but it seemed different now. He couldn't help wondering what Matthew would think of it… or what the kids would think. He could almost see Carl running through the house in his bathing suit and swimmies, ready to jump in the pool, or Will asking if it was okay for him to read in the shade of the cabana. Brianna would have dolls placed on the big living room chairs, and Gregory would bomb the carpet with Legos. Instead, the house looked like something out of a magazine or a set from a movie: beautiful, perfect, and lifeless.

He poured a drink and flopped into one of the chairs, then put his feet up. Ice tinkled in the glass as he sipped, and he sighed, then practically jumped at the doorbell. He wasn't expecting anyone, but then…. He set his glass on a coaster and got up to peer outside to see who was there.

"Couldn't you wait until tomorrow?" Lucas asked as he let Leon inside. "I got home an hour ago."

"Where's Karen? Don't you still have security? What about the guy stalking you?" Leon took off his jacket. "At least you're back and we can make arrangements so you'll have all the security you need to keep those kinds of people away from you." He wandered into the living room and poured himself a drink like he owned the place. "Everything is going to be fine now."

"Yes, it will. I'm all set to start filming on Monday." Lucas sat back down and picked up his drink, wanting to lure Leon in. "Karen has been very busy setting up a number of appointments for me for this week."

"I see. What kind of appointments? I'm going to need some time with you. There are a number of offers that have come in, and I want to talk them over with you. I have a couple of film projects that will be ready to begin next year, and there's a Netflix series that looks very promising. From what I can see, you are going to be very busy."

"So are you," Lucas retorted.

"I know. Keeping an eye on everything you're doing is going to take a lot of time." He actually smiled.

Lucas finished his drink. "That isn't what I mean. You're going to be busy in court, and you have plenty to answer for. Let's start with contacting Anthony—Ruetoyou—and forwarding him information on where I was going to be." He watched the shocked and put-upon expression. It was almost comical. Leon couldn't act for shit. "Before you deny it, although you covered your tracks really well, you got sloppy, and the bill for the airline ticket was sent to my business manager." He leaned forward. "What the hell were you trying to accomplish, anyway?"

Leon ground his jaw, and his eyes burned while his cheeks reddened. "I needed to get you back here."

"What? You were afraid I was going to stay there?"

Leon rolled his eyes. "Please. All it took was those first pictures of you playing with those kids and then the way you looked at that guy from high school and I knew I was right. You were falling for the guy. I could tell. I had to get you back here."

Lucas stood, took Leon's glass, and set it aside. "You were an idiot—a controlling, screwed-up idiot. But you did me a favor. See, I also messaged Marcus and had him review everything that you've submitted on my behalf, and he found a number of items that you had flagged that I had approved... but didn't." He hoped his gaze was withering.

"Of course you did," Leon countered. "You just don't remember."

Lucas shook his head. "I would remember authorizing you to take a trip to Paris, and as I remember, that was where you went on vacation last March. You asshole, charging that trip to me and thinking I wouldn't figure it out. Well, I have, and Bernie is in the process of charging back all improperly allocated expenses. All payments going forward will come to him, and he will pay you your cut less these expenses." Lucas's temper kept growing. "Oh, and in case you don't understand, you are fired. How dare you send someone to track me, and how dare you undermine my family, my friends, and me by telling anyone in the press where I am?" He heaved a deep breath.

"You know I'll sue," Leon said, his eyes raging.

"And if you do, then I'll present every shred of evidence to Anthony, my stalker. He'll make sure it gets reported, very publicly, how you ripped me off and had him follow me. How you even paid for his plane ticket. All of that will come to light. Not only will you have no reputation left, but you'll end up in jail." Lucas tapped him on the chest. "My thinking is that you should announce your retirement from this business and find something else to do." He was done. "See yourself out." He pointed and waited until Leon left the house before slumping in the chair.

He picked up his phone to call Karen, but remembered that he had given her the day off. Using the internet, he located a locksmith and requested immediate service. He'd change all the locks, and Bernie was already handling the accounting and financial pieces. Now he just needed a new agent, but he could start that process in the morning.

THE LIGHTS were out and the house was quiet. Lucas lay in bed, staring up at the ceiling. He checked the clock by the side of the bed and groaned. He had been home less than twelve hours and missed Matthew already. He rolled over in the empty king-size bed, wishing he could talk to Matthew, but it was early morning there, and he wasn't going to wake him. Instead, he got up and pulled on a robe. Opening the sliding glass doors, he slipped out into the warm night and down to the pool. After dropping the robe poolside, he slipped into the water and lay back, looking up at the light-polluted sky. What a difference from the sky back in Michigan, where the stars seemed so close he could touch them. Here everything seemed so far away.

After lying in the water for half an hour, he got out and pulled on his robe before going inside. It was nearly four in the morning, and he was tired now. He slid under the covers and fell asleep, only to wake a few hours later to his phone vibrating on the bedside table.

"Yes," he answered blearily.

"I heard you dumped your agent." It was Barry. Apparently word traveled fast.

"I did. He was stealing from me and was way too controlling." He left off the details. There was no need to spread those around. It was enough that the word was already spreading. "What can I do for you?"

"I need to run through some dialog edits. There are a few places where your voice didn't come through. Can you come in today? I know it's a long shot, but it will take an hour, tops, and allow us to move forward."

"Of course. Text me the address and I'll be there in, what… two hours?"

"Perfect. See you then."

Lucas ended the call and set the alarm to sleep for another half hour. Then he got himself up and went into the editing studio.

There was no one about, and the lights were on to say that recording was in progress, so he sat down to wait, knowing he was a little early. He checked messages as one came in from Matthew. It was him and the kids waving from in front of the beach house. *We left yesterday, and all the kids want to know if we can move there. They really liked it.*

It was fun, he sent. *I'm already at work. Need to do some vocals in a few places. No rest for the weary.* He pressed Send on the second message as Barry came out.

It was. We all miss you.

I miss you too, Lucas sent, and made sure it was on silent before shoving it into his pocket.

"Glad you could come," Barry said, shaking his hand and leading him into a darkened room with a huge television screen. "We have a list of about twelve places, and it's just a few lines."

"Got it," Lucas said. "Let's get this done so you can move on." He settled behind the prompter and ran through the lines easily. He had done this before on multiple occasions, so he was familiar with the routine. In less than an hour, he was done, and Barry was pleased.

"I have another project coming up in about a year or so. It's a smaller film, more intimate, but the lead is perfect for you, if you're interested. It's not the huge budgets you usually get."

Lucas nodded. "Send the details directly to me. I'm going to have to be my own agent until I find one who doesn't make me want to pull my hair out." He was being overly dramatic, but Leon had hurt him. Lucas had trusted the guy and had been betrayed.

"I understand." Barry reached into his bag and pulled out a card. "Look into her. Lesley's bright, and she's been working with a number of younger people. She's been around for over a decade, and she seems to really know what she's doing. Also, she answers her phone and returns calls." In their business, that was half the battle.

"Thank you." Lucas slipped the card into his pocket.

"Something has changed," Barry said. "I can't put my finger on what, but you seem different. I don't want to say less driven, but maybe more settled." He clapped Lucas on the shoulder. "I know you were away because of your father's passing. Was that it?"

Lucas shrugged. "My father and I made some sort of peace before he passed, but no. I think a lot of the things I really want have come into focus."

Barry smiled brightly. "This business is a pain the ass most of the time. It has its ups, and kid, right now you are on top. But it doesn't always stay that way. You'll suddenly be out of favor and have no idea why, or you won't get a part you're perfect for because the producer wants someone with blond hair and the carpet has to match the curtains. You never know. So whatever helped bring things into perspective, I'm glad for it. Decide what you want, especially if it has nothing to do with this business. If you make movies your life, in the end all you'll have is that beam of light between the projector and the screen. It makes things look beautiful, but it has no real substance."

"Thanks." Sometimes Lucas wondered if he was surrounded by philosophers, but Barry had a real point. They shook hands, and Barry walked him to the door.

"I'll send that script and the project details directly to you, and we can work together until you get a new agent."

Lucas left the studio, slipping his hand in his pocket, fingering the business card. In the car, he started the engine and pulled out the card, staring at the number before placing a call.

"UNCLE DADDY, I wanna talk too." Lucas heard Carl in the background.

"You can say hello in a few minutes," Matthew said, and Lucas chuckled. "So things went well with Lesley?"

"Yeah, they seemed to. I'm on my way to meet and go over where I am and the type of roles that I'm interested in going forward. I explained what I had on my schedule and the projects I was considering." He'd also explained the changes he was thinking of making. "I've been home just a few days, and already I feel like everything has been turned upside down and I'm trying to put the pieces back together."

Matthew sighed. "Same here. The plant is going to close after this season. I had a meeting with a representative of the new owners. They were impressed with the work I've been doing and offered me a job at a location in Cincinnati, Ohio."

"God. That's quite a move," Lucas said.

"Yeah, and I don't know what I'm going to do. It will mean that I'll have to move the kids, but there's no guarantee of how long that job will last. They aren't saying, but with the way that these food processing plants consolidate, I expect that this new job won't last too long either. I'm thinking of starting my own business as an electrical contractor. I can work in residential or commercial spaces because of my experience." He sounded so low, and Lucas wished he could help.

Lucas pulled to a stop in traffic, tapping the wheel.

"What's wrong?" Matthew asked. "The tapping."

"I'm trying to ignore the people in the car next to me, who have recognized me and are pointing and waving." Lucas waved back, and thankfully his lane pulled ahead and he was able to exit the freeway. He took Sepulveda down to the office building. "They're gone." He parked on the street and sat in the car.

"I'm going to switch to Facetime," Matthew said, and Lucas picked up the phone. All the kids sat on the sofa, waving.

"I drawed you a picture," Brianna said, hurrying up so she could show him on the camera. "It's all of us at the beach."

Lucas's throat ached. "It's beautiful." Matthew asked her to sit back down, and Carl waved.

"I learned how to swim." He did his motions. "Oh, and I hate day camp." He made a face, and Will rolled his eyes.

"That's because there are mostly girls there."

"One tried to kiss me," Carl said, wiping his cheek, which made Lucas laugh.

"I'm going to play basketball," Gregory said. "Uncle Daddy is going to take me to a camp where I can learn to be better."

"You'll be awesome. I know it. What about you, Will?" Lucas asked, and the oldest shrugged. He knew what Will liked. "I sent your Uncle Daddy an Amazon gift card for all of you so you can all get some books, okay?" Will perked up. Nothing spoke to that boy like stories. "And I'll read one to you all soon over the phone." Damn, he missed these kids.

"Say goodbye," Matthew prompted, and after waves and a chorus of goodbyes, the phone returned to voice. "I'll talk to you soon."

"Looking forward to it. Monday I start filming, but I'll send you a few pictures and things." He couldn't help feeling sad when the call disconnected, but he needed to go or he'd be late for the meeting.

Lucas got a few looks inside the building, but he paid no attention, instead going right up to the eighth floor. The agency took up one side, and he walked in.

"Mr. Reardon."

"Lucas," he corrected, and the receptionist smiled.

"Lesley is waiting for you in the conference room. Please go right in." She motioned to the next door as the phone rang. He thanked her and went on down.

"Lucas," she said, standing up as he entered. She was small, thin, elegant in her business suit, with eyes as piercing and intense as any he had ever seen. Then she smiled, and damn, he would be willing to give her just about anything if she asked for it. "I'm so glad you called." She moved to a set of upholstered chairs in the corner, and Lucas sat and got comfortable. "I heard about Leon, and I want you to know there will be nothing like that if you decide to go with us. We are a professional organization, and we keep detailed records and issue regular reports. Nothing is ever hidden."

"That's good to know."

"Secondly, what I'd like to do is talk about how you see yourself. I know you're at the top of your game right now and you have a number of contracts already, and those will stay with Leon, although we will administer them. There is no way we will leave you hanging."

"True. But there are a number of unsigned projects in the works, and I want to transfer all of them. I don't expect you to go into this for nothing." He leaned forward. "But…."

She nodded. "Go ahead."

"I don't really know. I think I'd like to have a life."

Lesley sat back. "I agree. We need to do a better job of picking the projects you'll take on. Leon seemed to accept everything that was offered, and that isn't helping you. Overexposure is possible, and we don't want that. So what we're going to do is pick and choose two, maybe three projects a year, and those we'll put everything we have into. The rest we'll take a pass on. The exception is something too good to pass up. But those will be few and far between." She smiled again. "Frankly, you look tired."

"I took a few weeks off and got some rest, but this whole thing with Leon has me at loose ends. I need some stability and someone who isn't pulling at me all the time."

"Exactly. If you decide to go with us, we will be in your corner all the way… and yet we will not be part of your life. My goal is to be like the electric company, working for you, but in the background. I'll work the deals, we'll talk them over, take the ones you like, and then you are freed up to do what you do best. I'm not going to show up on set or pop around to your house unless I'm invited or you need me. I don't work that way. You need to be free to be creative and have a life of your own. It's my job to take care of all the Hollywood bullshit." This almost seemed too good to be true. "What I'd like to do is send over a copy of our agency agreement. You look it over and we'll talk about it."

"Is that all?" Lucas asked.

Lesley shrugged. "What more do you want me to say? I could fangirl all over the place or blow smoke up your ass, but that isn't going to get either of us anywhere. I'm a straightforward, down-to-earth person, and I'll tell you what I think. To the people we're negotiating with, I'll be the bulldog from hell when necessary." Lucas liked that. "But most importantly, you need to be comfortable with what we're doing. Look over what I gave you and take your time."

Lucas was about to stand, but he thought of a few more things. "There are some changes that I'm thinking of making. I want a family, but I don't want to bring them up here."

She sat back. "Are you asking me if you can live somewhere else? There are actors who live all over the country. Most stick to either the east or west coast, but it's possible, especially if we plan your travel and ease up a little on your workload. But don't go into this with any illusions. You will need to travel to location or even here in LA for work at the studio." She placed her hands on the table. "My advice would be to keep a house here in town as well as one where you want to live. The last thing you want is to be staying in a hotel for months while you work here. I'd also suggest that you make sure the house is big enough so your family can come here with you sometimes."

"I hadn't thought of that."

"I take it the family you're thinking of already exists."

Lucas nodded. "I reconnected with an old boyfriend when I went home. He's raising his sister's three boys and her daughter. He was my first love...."

"And you never forgot him," Lesley filled in.

Lucas leaned forward. "It's more than that. Matthew knew and loved me before I was the famous Lucas Reardon. He knows me for me and loves the person, not the image on the screen."

Lesley smiled. "There are a couple of things I have learned. First is that actors who have a stable and fulfilling family life are happiest, and their careers last longer. But second, finding someone who knows you for who you are is hard out in the real world. In Hollywood, it's a fucking pink unicorn in go-go boots. If what the two of you feel is real, then hold on to it. Stars meet, marry, fight, split, and divorce every single day. But the real stories in this town are those couples who stay together for twenty, thirty, or forty years." Damn, from those sharp eyes, it seemed she knew exactly what she was talking about. Lucas wanted her in his corner.

"Thank you." He stood, and shook her hand when she did the same. "I really appreciate your candor. I'm going to look these over, and I'll have my attorney do the same. We'll definitely be back in touch." He liked Lesley and could see working with her for a long time.

With a plan for that part of his life, Lucas now needed to figure out the rest, and that was going to be more complicated.

CHAPTER 14

SUMMER WAS waning, and Matthew was nearing the end of the plant's busiest time of year. The final loads of beans had been processed weeks ago, and they were about to shift over to corn. From there, they would finish out the year, and then the equipment that he had babied along for years would be dismantled and sent away. It would be hard for him to make that shift in his life, but he was already preparing. Matthew checked the time and got ready to leave.

On the way home, he stopped at Mrs. Livingston's in town and spent about an hour repairing the electrical outlets in her kitchen, which hadn't been wired correctly in the first place. He was almost done, and with the kids in their last week of day camp, he took the extra time to finish the last of the work for her. She'd been patient, letting him work on the project as he got time, and the check she handed him would go right in the bank toward his new business.

"I appreciate your patience," he told the retiree with white hair. She always had a quick smile, and just like every time he worked there, she handed him a plastic container of cookies for the kids.

"Now I can sleep at night and not worry that the toaster is going to try to take over the world." She saw him to the door, and Matthew thanked her again before heading out to the family SUV, putting his tools in the very back, then hurrying to pick up the kids. He was already on the verge of being late, but he got there just in time to keep from incurring the wrath of the camp director, and the fine for being late.

"Did you have a good day?"

"Carl pooped himself," Brianna reported as she got herself in her booster seat.

"You're such a tattletale," Gregory said, coming to his brother's defense. "It was just a little, and they came and got me and I helped him get cleaned up. Will was busy playing with Melissa Carter."

"Now who's tattling?" Matthew said flatly as he made sure all the kids were buckled in.

"Sorry, Uncle Daddy," Gregory said.

Matthew nodded and patted his second son's leg. "You did good helping your brother. Thank you." There were days when he wondered how he'd make it through if it weren't for those two. They had started taking on more chores around the house, and as a result, they both got an allowance.

"Are you okay, Uncle Daddy?" Brianna asked. "You look sad."

Matthew forced a smile. These kids didn't need to deal with his problems. His job ending at the plant had placed added stress on him, and if he was honest, he was lonely. Those few weeks in the summer with Lucas had given him a glimpse into what it could be like with someone he loved in his life. Letting Lucas go had been one of the hardest things he had ever done. Matthew knew he had been right, but weeks of an empty bed and vivid, often lurid dreams starring his favorite actor only enhanced the emptiness once he woke. "I'm okay, sweetheart, I promise." One way or another, he would be.

"You're sure?" Brianna was a dear when she wasn't telling tales.

"Yes, sweetheart." He had to be. Each call with Lucas lifted his spirits and brought a smile. He'd gotten pictures that he kept on his phone—pictures of Lucas on the set, a few from the pool, and one of him in the shower that the tabloids would kill for. That one was password protected, his favorite… all that wet, glowing skin and those dreamy, come-hither eyes…. Matthew pushed those thoughts away. This was not the time.

"Can we go out for dinner?" Will asked. "We're all really hungry." The way he asked made it sound like he expected a no.

Matthew was exhausted as well. "Where do you want to go?"

All the kids looked at each other like they were checking. "Dairy Barn… moooo," Carl said and then laughed at his own joke. Sometimes four-year-olds were weird.

"Okay," Matthew agreed and pulled out of the lot.

"WHO'S HERE?" Will asked as Matthew pulled into the driveway back at the house. He parked next to a dark blue Escape with an Enterprise sticker.

Matthew got out as the driver's door opened. Lucas came around the back of the car.

Matthew could hardly believe his eyes. He blinked more than once just to make sure this wasn't some dream his lonely mind had cooked up. "You're here." It sounded lame, even to his own ears, but those were the only words that came out. "What? Why didn't you tell me?"

"I wanted it to be a surprise," Lucas said, standing right in front of him.

"It was." Matthew swallowed, not daring to move in case this was some daylight fantasy that would pop at the slightest touch. "Are you real?"

Lucas reached out, lightly touching his cheeks. Matthew started at the first sensation of those warm hands, letting them draw him closer until Lucas kissed him.

Everything seemed to happen at once. When Matthew realized this was well and truly real, he kissed Lucas back, wrapping him in a bear hug of epic proportions, and finally, as the kiss came to an end, he heard the kids cheering from inside the car. Well, mostly cheers and one "eeeew, kissing," but he could live with that.

"What are you doing here?" Matthew asked once he stood in Lucas's arms, sighing as the tension seemed to flow out of him. "You're supposed to be working."

"I got a week off. They don't need me for the next scenes, so I got the heck out of Dodge." He pulled back.

"So you're just here to visit," Matthew said.

Lucas smiled. "You and I have a lot to talk about. But I'm not going to do any of it standing outside in full view of the kids." He winked, and Matthew's mind slipped into gear. He backed away and got the kids out of the car, with each of them vying for some of Lucas's attention.

"All of you go on inside," Matthew told them, and they trooped up to the door. Matthew let everyone into the house, and they fanned out. "Take care of your things, and then you all need baths or showers before bed." He made sure the kids got going. "Do you need anything?"

Lucas shook his head. "Get the kids ready and settled."

Carl raced down the hall and into the room, naked. "Will you read to us?" he asked Lucas.

"Yes, but you have to have your bath first and then get your jammies on. Then I'll read you a story with all the voices."

Carl hurried back to the bathroom, and Matthew took a second to kiss Lucas before following Carl to get him into the tub.

Bath time was always hectic, but Matthew found he had less patience than usual. Fortunately, the kids were tired, and after his story, Carl went right to sleep. The others finally fell quiet, and Matthew joined Lucas in the living room, picking up blankets and putting toys away.

"There's nothing to be nervous about," Lucas said.

"Sure there is. You came all this way for a few days, and then you're going to leave again." He blinked a few times and shook his head to try to get his jitters under control. "You and I can't keep on like this, I know that, and I figured that you came back because you need to move on."

Lucas took the stuffed dog from his hand and put it aside. "I came here because I figured a few things out."

"Like what?" Matthew asked softly, waiting for the bad news.

"Well, like I want to make my home here. You're right, it isn't fair to ask the kids to give up their life and move all across the country, and truth be told, I don't want to live there either. I'm happy here, and I want to build a life… here… with you… all of you. I have commitments, but my new agent and I have worked up a framework where I won't be doing as many films. I want time with you, the kids—time for us to build a family… together."

Matthew had to have heard wrong. "Are you kidding me? This is what I've dreamed of, and… shit like that doesn't happen to me."

"Yes, you heard me. The house that we stayed in a few months ago was up for sale, so I bought it. The closing is pending, but yeah. I bought a house here. Without Rachel and Karen, there's enough room for each of the kids to have their own room and you and I to have a suite of our own. I also thought we could add a workshop onto the garage so you would have a place to base your business out of. I'm also going to have a fence built around the property for security… and then I figure the kids can get a dog and…. What is it?"

Matthew rubbed his eyes. "You bought the place without asking me?"

"Yeah." Lucas said gently. "I thought it would make a good wedding present, eventually. I wanted to show you that I was serious. There are going to be times when I'm going to have to travel and be away, I know that, but I want you to know that when I come home, it will be to you… in our house… here."

"But what about your place out there? How are you going to get back and forth?" A million questions just popped into his head, which was running a mile a minute. "Wait, hold that…. Are you asking me to marry you?"

"Well, yeah." Lucas rolled his eyes. "I want you in my life always. And I want all of us to be a family. You, me, Carl, Brianna, Gregory, and Will… probably a bunch of dogs, cats, fish, and goodness knows what else. So yes…." Lucas went down on one knee. "I didn't get you a ring, but I did buy a house, so I hope that acts as a stand-in. So Matthew, I never want to be without you in my life. I want to go to bed with you and wake up next to you, raise a family, and have a full life… with you. Will you marry me?"

He was almost too shocked to move, but finally he smiled. He began to laugh and cry at the same damn time. "You bought us a house?"

"Well… yeah. And I want you and the kids to come out to California as soon as you can. I'm going to sell my house out there and buy one that we can all stay in. I'm going to have to work out there quite a bit, so I thought when the kids aren't in school, we can stay there. But you and I will make here, this place—our house—a home."

Matthew could barely believe his ears. "Is this really what you want?"

Lucas nodded. "More than anything. I want to have friends and surround ourselves with people who care about us. I want the kids to have a life filled with horses and summers on the lake, winters with snow. I want them to have the best lives we can give them." He hugged Matthew tightly. "Mostly I want to love you until the day I die. If nothing else, I know that will make me happy. The rest is icing on the cake."

This was too much to take in. "You're really willing to give up your life out there?" He knew how hard Lucas had worked and how much it meant to him.

"I'm not giving up anything. If you agree to be with me, then I'm getting everything."

Matthew nodded, trying to think of something to say, but he came up empty.

"I have just one more thing. Can I get an answer so I can get up off my knees?"

Matthew chuckled. "Yes" was all he could manage. Lucas stood, cradling his cheeks in his hands; then he pulled Matthew down into a gentle kiss. "Come on." Matthew took Lucas by the hand and led him down toward the bedroom, then closed and locked the door behind them. "You're really up for this?"

Lucas pushed him down on the bed. Then, with a single movement, he tugged his shirt over his head, revealing acres of honey-warm skin that Matthew had dreamed about ever since Lucas left. He swallowed and was about to sit up, but Lucas shook his head as he kicked off his shoes and shed the last of his clothes.

"I'm up for anything, sweetheart," he whispered before joining Matthew on the bed to celebrate their engagement.

EPILOGUE

"UNCLE PAPA, do you really have to go?" Carl asked, looking up at him with those big blue eyes. Lucas knew the five-year-old had him wrapped around his little finger. Damn, every time he called him that, Lucas wanted to give the little scamp anything he wanted.

"I do, buddy. They need me back in Hollywood because tomorrow is the opening of *Superboy 2* and everyone wants to see me fly again." He turned to Matthew, who nodded.

"I'm gonna miss you," Carl said, running over for a hug, which Lucas readily gave.

"But you don't have to." He lifted Carl into his arms. "Because you're all going with me. Uncle Daddy wanted it to be a surprise. We have to leave in an hour. Uncle Daddy already packed your stuff."

Carl put his arms around his neck. "Really?" He fidgeted, and when Lucas put him down, Carl ran out and down to his room under the stairs. Lucas had originally thought it would make a good workout room and office for him, but it ended up as Carl's bedroom so that he would be on the same level as him and Matthew.

"We're really going to a movie premiere?" Gregory asked.

Matthew grinned. Lucas loved making him smile. Nothing set his heart racing like that expression. It had for the past year, and Lucas hoped to get that reaction for the rest of their lives. "Yes. Lucas and I already worked it all out, and since the last day of school was yesterday, we're going to spend two weeks at the house in LA. Lucas has the premiere and some work to do, and then we're all going to Disneyland."

Carl came back, and Lucas doubled over. He'd pulled on his arm swimmies. "I'm ready to go." The water in early June wasn't warm enough to swim in, but apparently their own water baby remembered about the pool.

"I already packed your suit and a set of swimmies for you to take, and everything else you'll need. So put those back so you have them when we get home." Matthew could be stern, where Lucas just couldn't seem to manage it. "Rachel will be back in a few minutes, and we need to be ready. So get your shoes on and light jackets. She's going to drive us to the airport, and then we'll be on our way." Rachel had taken a job providing security for the house here in Michigan, as well as keeping their family safe in LA. Definitely a full-time job. The kids all took off to make sure they had everything, and Matthew moved into Lucas's arms.

"You owe me twenty bucks," Matthew said. "I kept it a secret and even managed to pack for them without giving it away." He smiled, and Lucas kissed him hard, wanting more but unable to have it right now.

"I owe you a heck of a lot more than that." The past year had been amazing. Lucas had spent more time away than he wanted, but after a lot of work and flights home whenever he could, his schedule was manageable now, and he spent more time at home. There were a lot of work sessions and Zoom conferences, but he could live with those as long as once they were over, he got to walk out of the office he'd added to the side of the house and be with Matthew and the kids. He had previously lived for his career. Now he had something much more important to spend his time and energy on.

"Rachel is here," Brianna reported as she hurried back. To his surprise, the kids were dressed and ready, except for Carl, who had decided he was hot and returned in only his underwear. Matthew got him dressed again while Lucas and the others helped Rachel load the car. Then Lucas, Matthew, and their entire family set off on a new adventure. Hollywood needed to look out, because the Reardon-Wilsons were coming, and the town was never going to be the same.

Keep reading for an Excerpt from
New Leaf
by Andrew Grey.

AFTER HOURS of talking and listening, Dex was worn out, and the time change was getting to him. Fortunately, he found Jane.

"Go for a walk. This will go on until the funeral. Your mother was loved, but it's going to be overwhelming if you don't take a break." She smiled. "Take the keys to the store if you want."

Dex gratefully went out the back door and through the yard, weaving along the back alley to the store. Then, after unlocking the rear door, he let himself inside.

The familiar scent of dust, books, and his mother nearly sent him reeling. This he remembered. Dex closed the door and turned on the lights as he wandered through the small back room with its boxes and shelves. His mother didn't keep much back here. She never had. She'd always said that she couldn't sell what was back here, so she kept as much of her stock out front as possible. Dex perused the area, remembering the corner where she'd set up a table and chairs. He had sat there for hours doing his homework, coloring, crafts—all of it in his own corner of the store. Oh, the hours he'd spent in this space with his mom. She always came back to check on him, and if there was no one in the store, she'd read to him or they'd color together until the bell on the front door jangled. It got to the point that he hated that bell because it meant she'd have to go back to work.

He peeked into some of the boxes before stepping through the curtain and out behind the register. The lights were off, but the sun shone in through the front windows. Everything looked as though his mother would return at any moment to open up. The shelves were all in order, and even the notebook she kept on the counter behind the register sat in its usual spot, surrounded by the trinkets and bookmark display. Dex lifted the counter and lowered it again once he'd stepped out from behind it, then wandered the aisles, looking over the rack of children's books. His mother had read most of them to him at one point. Of course, there were newer ones as well, but he continued on, checking over the shelves.

More books were turned cover forward to fill the shelves than he remembered. When he was a kid, the store had always been packed. But now it seemed staged—behind the single titles, there was nothing. The inventory he remembered his mother carrying wasn't in the store. Maybe it was just the children's section?

He continued to the adult areas of the store. There he found only a few hardcover books, and of the titles she had, his mother only had two or three copies. Dex knew independent bookstores had been having a difficult time in the past years because of Amazon, but every time he had asked his mother how the store was, she had told him it was fine. Maybe things hadn't been as rosy as his mother projected.

A knock on the front door startled him. He went up front, turned the lock, and opened the door. "Can I help you? We're closed for the next few days."

"I'm sorry. I was just passing, and I always stop by when I'm downtown." The man lifted his gaze, and Dex was struck by the most intensely blue eyes he had ever seen.

"My mother passed away and…." Damn, it was hard just to say the words. "The store will be closed until after the funeral." He put his hand over his mouth, willing himself not to fall apart. He had been okay a few minutes ago, but the grief was suddenly too much to bear.

"I'm so sorry. She was a nice lady." He paused, lowering his gaze slightly, looking like he might leave. "You're Sarah's son? She talked a lot about you. She said you were going to be in the movies." He smiled.

Dex swallowed hard. His mind skipped to how hunkalicious this guy was, with his hair all askew and his wrinkled shirt open just enough to allow Dex to catch a glimpse of a smattering of brown chest hair.

"Yes. I'm Dex." It was nice that his mom had talked about him. Even if he hadn't had any real success in Hollywood, his mother had always been proud of him anyway, he thought, his heart hitching.

"I was a regular customer of your mom's. I try to support local businesses, and she'd order in the books I wanted. That way she got the business instead of the big online places." He smiled, and Dex nodded.

"Did she have an order for you?" He wondered where his mother might have put it if she had.

"No. There were a few books I wanted, though. Still, I can come back once you're open again…." He leaned closer. "You are opening again, aren't you?" The blue in his eyes grew darker. "This is the only place in town that would order books for me. At least, the ones I wanted." He looked up and down the street. "I've got a weakness for romance— the masculine kind."

"I see…."

He put his hand over his mouth. "Of course. Sarah told me she had a gay son." He cleared his throat. "I'm sorry. I'm Les. Les Gable." He shook his hand. "I'm sorry to keep you. I'll come back later." He paused. "I just want to tell you that your mom was the greatest. She cared so much about everyone. I'm going to miss her." Then he turned and, with a wave, hurried down the sidewalk.

Dex closed the door and locked it again. It seemed his mother had had an impact on a lot of people in town. She had always loved books and got a great deal of joy from reading, something she had passed on to Dex.

He walked through the store before returning to the back room. He found the safe where his mother always kept it, and searched his memory for the combination. She had told him what it was years ago, and luckily the numbers returned to him. He opened it and peered inside, where he found less than a hundred dollars, her starting bank for the day. He also pulled out the store accounts book. Then he closed the safe door and locked it again.

He wasn't sure what else he wanted to do, but he didn't want to go back to the house. The grief gathering was probably still going on, and he'd had enough. His mother was gone, and Dex needed to try to process the loss alone. He didn't need dozens of people talking about his mother for him to know her. His mom was here in this building—in each book, as well as in the way she'd painted each wall a different color because she thought it would be cheerful. The only problem was that she'd picked the brightest colors possible. Dex was afraid his eyes would start bleeding if he didn't do something about it soon. Especially that grass-green carpeting. "Mom, I love you, but your decorating was a nightmare," he said out loud, smiling. That was his mother. She loved what she loved, and to hell with what everyone else thought.

Dex set down the books and headed for the bathroom, gasping when he opened the door. Apparently where the bathroom in the house was Whoville, the one in the store was all Alice in Wonderland, and it had gotten the same treatment, including a Mad Hatter toilet-paper holder and a Queen of Hearts toilet cozy. The White Rabbit bounded over one of the walls, but it was Alice being sucked down the rabbit hole that made him laugh. It came with a reminder to flush. This was his mother in a nutshell. She could be out there, and yet she could also be so clever.

He shut the door, unable to use the bathroom, and retrieved the record book. It was time to go back to the house. At least now he could review his mom's records and figure out if it was viable to keep the store going.

He had a task to accomplish, something that would fill some hours and keep him from moping around. If the store was his mother's legacy, Dex needed to see if there was a way to move forward. He pulled open the rear door and locked it behind him, then headed back toward the house.

He decided to take a roundabout route, walking down to the square as the clock in the old courthouse chimed the hour. He paused and smiled. He remembered being in the store, listening for that bell, because most days, when it chimed six times, his mom would close up and they would go home. He shook his head as if to clear the memories. Something around every corner seemed to remind him of her. The trees had all leafed out, shading the streets. Dex wiped his eyes. In his mind's eye, he could see his mom and dad in their backyard, music drifting out from the house as they danced to a cascade of flower petals.

At the time, he'd considered it horribly embarrassing, especially when his mother had backed away from his dad insisting that she teach Dex to dance. Dex had fought it with everything he had. He hadn't wanted to learn to dance. But she'd made him. Damn, what he wouldn't give to dance with her with one last time.

"Dex?"

He turned and once again met Les's blue eyes. His heart beat a little faster and his throat dried in an instant, especially seeing the heat and interest in those eyes. Dex was used to people looking at him with hunger, but this was something more. "I just left the library and was on my way back to my apartment. What are you up to?"

"I finished up in the store and figured it was time to go home." He nodded in the direction he was going, and Les fell into step along with him, walking slowly. Dex realized that his one leg seemed stiff. He shortened his usual stride so Les wouldn't have to strain to keep up.

Les smiled at him. "Sarah always told me stories about you when I was in the store. She said that you're an actor working in LA."

"I haven't been working all that much lately, unfortunately. Unless you count porn," Dex said, his voice deadpan.

Les stopped midstride. "You did porn?"

Dex shook his head, grinning. "Oh God, no. My last audition was supposed to be a serious role, but well, it didn't turn out that way. My mother was always supportive, but I can't help but think her support would not stretch to cover that." He chuckled. "Though maybe Mom would have just told me to do my best, then rented a copy later so she could tell me what I'd done wrong." He chuckled. "I would have to say that the most embarrassing thing I can think of is my mother going out to get a copy of Shaving Ryan's Privates or something, so she could rate my performance."

Les chuckled. "It must have been nice to have that kind of support in your life. I never did. My family wasn't anywhere near as open-minded as your mom, that's for sure. My folks were very predictable. 'You will go to college, you will go to church, you will not be gay or have gay thoughts.'" The humor left his voice and his posture became more rigid when he spoke of his parents.

Dex had always known he'd been lucky, especially when it came to his mom, but he sometimes forgot how fortunate. "I never knew how Mom was going to take anything. You remember what it was like to be a teenager and all you wanted to do was shock your parents? I'd do that, and Mom would look at me and say, 'It's okay, I support you and will always love you.' Then the next day she'd decide that the upstairs bathroom needed painting and I'd walk in and get a surprise of my own when the walls were jet black... or neon yellow. The hall bathroom upstairs has been both at one time. I think it was her way of shocking me right back. And her offbeat decorating skills usually did the trick."

Les laughed out loud, his stance loosening. "She would do the funniest things. One time when I came into the store, she had the shelves pulled back from one of the walls and was painting it Barbie pink, just so she could see how it would look."

"That's my mom," Dex agreed.

"At least she liked color. My mother painted the entire house this off-white color. She called it Palest Peony or something, and every wall in every room was the same color, all through the house. I had to beg her to let me do my room in blue. She eventually let me, but only if I promised that if it didn't work out, I'd paint it back. The furniture was every shade of brown, and the carpet beige. It was like living in a forest in permanent winter. Mom's idea of adding color was bringing in black accents... because they went with everything." Les began to laugh. "My dad hated it. So for Christmas, he used to get her really bright knickknacks. They would be on display for a while and then suddenly they'd disappear." He smiled.

"You're kidding, right?" Dex asked. When Les shook his head, Dex added, "You should see the guest bedroom upstairs. It has this psychedelic wallpaper, as if the person who created it had done acid back in the sixties. I have no idea where Mom found it, but I'm surprised anyone who's stayed over hasn't suffered from seizures." He paused. "You know, that could be why Mom didn't get many guests. They'd stay one night and detour to the hospital on their way out of town."

Les shrugged, smiling. "You know what they say—after three days, both fish and guests begin to stink. Maybe it was her way of controlling the odor." He tilted his head adorably to the side, and Dex took a second to enjoy the view. Les had a strong jaw and an expressive face that pulled Dex in. His high cheekbones gave him an almost regal look, and yet his eyes danced with mischief. And he had a sense of humor, which was necessary… if just to get through the trials and tribulations of life. Dex had definitely needed one with his mother. She had sometimes been a handful.

"My mom's guest room…."

"Let me guess, slightly pinky off-white," Dex teased.

"Yup. I remember having a friend for a sleepover. I showed him into the room—he set down his bag and fell onto the bed, asleep instantly." He grinned and Dex rolled his eyes before chuckling lightly.

"So your mom was color-challenged. And mine was a color ninja, never afraid of anything." They approached the house, and Dex groaned as a couple went inside carrying a casserole dish. "I swear to God, the house is going to explode with all the grief food people are bringing." He patted his stomach, which did a little roll at the thought. "Want to hazard a guess as to the number of pounds of macaroni and cans of soup that have given their lives already?"

Les shook his head vehemently. "Not on your life." He patted Dex's shoulder, and heat spread through him from the touch. "I need to get home too. But I'll see you later at the store?" His gaze met Dex's, and Dex nodded but made no effort to move away. There was something incredibly attractive about being lost in those eyes, and he was in no hurry to return to reality. Les licked his lips, and just like that, Dex wondered how he tasted. Les was a feast for the eyes, and his musky scent wafted on the breeze. Dex swallowed hard, wishing for more, but there were limits to what he'd do with a guy he'd just met.

It was bad enough that Dex had done things he could never tell his mother in order to try to secure a role. He suppressed a shiver thinking about it. This wasn't Hollywood. Les was just a handsome guy. "I should go inside and make sure Jane isn't overwhelmed."

Les nodded, and Dex shook his hand, then forced himself to turn away from him and walk inside the house.

SCAN THE QR CODE
BELOW TO PREORDER!

ANDREW GREY is the author of more than two hundred works of Contemporary Gay Romantic fiction, including an Amazon Editors Best Romance of 2023. After twenty-seven years in corporate America, he has now settled down in Central Pennsylvania with his husband of more than twenty-five years, Dominic, and his laptop. An interesting ménage. Andrew grew up in western Michigan with a father who loved to tell stories and a mother who loved to read them. Since then he has lived throughout the country and traveled throughout the world. He is a recipient of the RWA Centennial Award, has a master's degree from the University of Wisconsin–Milwaukee, and now writes full-time. Andrew's hobbies include collecting antiques, gardening, and leaving his dirty dishes anywhere but in the sink (particularly when writing). He considers himself blessed with an accepting family, fantastic friends, and the world's most supportive and loving partner. Andrew currently lives in beautiful, historic Carlisle, Pennsylvania.

Email:andrewgrey@comcast.net

Website:www.andrewgreybooks.com

Follow me on BookBub

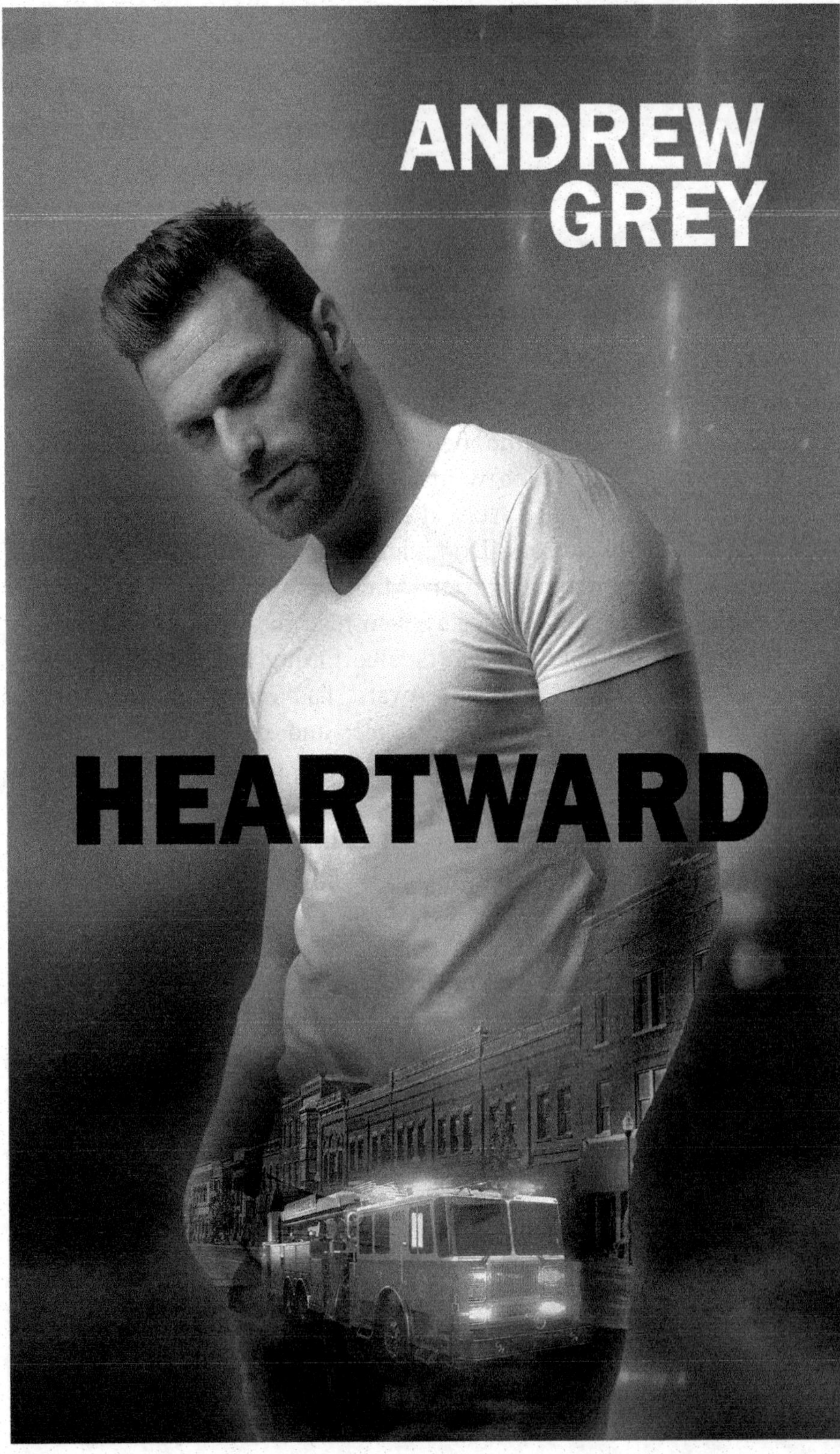
ANDREW
GREY
HEARTWARD

He doesn't know that home is where his heart will be....

Firefighter Tyler Banik has seen his share of adventure while working disaster relief with the Red Cross. But now that he's adopted Abey, he's ready to leave the danger behind and put down roots. That means returning to his hometown—where the last thing he anticipates is falling for his high school nemesis.

Alan Pettaprin isn't the boy he used to be. As a business owner and council member, he's working hard to improve life in Scottville for everyone. Nobody is more surprised than Alan when Tyler returns, but he's glad. For him, it's a chance to set things right. Little does he guess he and Tyler will find the missing pieces of themselves in each other. Old rivalries are left in the ashes, passion burns bright, and the possibility for a future together stretches in front of them....

But not everyone in town is glad to see Tyler return....

SCAN THE QR CODE
BELOW TO PREORDER!

ONLY THE BRIGHTEST STARS

ANDREW GREY

The problem with being an actor on top of the world is that you have a long way to fall.

Logan Steele is miserable. Hollywood life is dragging him down. Drugs, men, and booze are all too easy. Pulling himself out of his self-destructive spiral, not so much.

Brit Stimple does whatever he can to pay the bills. Right now that means editing porn. But Brit knows he has the talent to make it big, and he gets his break one night when Logan sees him perform on stage.

When Logan arranges for an opportunity for Brit to prove his talent, Brit's whole life turns around. Brit's talent shines brightly for all to see, and he brings joy and love to Logan's life and stability to his out-of-control lifestyle. Unfortunately, not everyone is happy for Logan, and as Brit's star rises, Logan's demons marshal forces to try to tear the new lovers apart.

SCAN THE QR CODE
BELOW TO PREORDER!

A NEW LEAF 🌿 ROMANCE

IN THE
WEEDS
ANDREW GREY

Florist to the stars Vin Robins is in high demand in LA, but he hates working for someone else. When he returns to his Pennsylvania home to help his widowed father, he finds an opportunity he never expected with his first love, but learns that someone's been taking advantage of the unused family greenhouse.

Casey Lombard wasted too much of his life denying who he is and what he wants, but he won't do that any longer. His biggest regret is letting Vin go, so running into Vin again when he gets called to investigate who planted pot on Vin's family's property sends him reeling.

Vin ignites feelings Casey thought long dead. But Casey has a daughter, and Vin is only home for a visit. Surely the bright lights of Hollywood will call him back to the City of Angels, so how can Vin and Casey build the life they both wish they had?

SCAN THE QR CODE BELOW TO PREORDER!

ANDREW GREY
Rescue Me

Everybody needs to be rescued sometime.

Veterinarian Mitchell Brannigan gets off to a rocky start with his new neighbor when someone calls the town to complain about the noise. Mitchell runs a shelter for rescue dogs, and dogs bark. But when he goes to make peace, he meets Beau Pfister and his fussy baby daughter, Jessica… and starts to fall in love.

Beau moved out to the country to get away from his abusive ex-husband, but raising an infant alone, with no support network, is lonely and exhausting. The last thing he expects is a helping hand from the neighbor whose dogs he complained about.

Mitchell understands what it's like to live in fear of your ex, and he's determined to help Beau move on. But when an unseen menace threatens the shelter and Beau, it becomes apparent that he hasn't dealt with his own demons.

With each other and a protective Chihuahua for support, Mitchell, Beau, and Jessica could make a perfect family. Mitchell won't let anything happen to them.

But who's going to rescue him?

SCAN THE QR CODE
BELOW TO PREORDER!

Everyone needs to be rescued sometimes.

As a vet tech, Daniel is usually first in line to come to animals' aid. When he and his boss get a call about an animal hoarding situation, they expect the handful of badly treated dogs... but the tiger comes as a surprise.

Wes recently left his job to care for his sick mother. Now that she's on the mend, he needs work, and he finds it at a bustling shelter. But the animals aren't the only ones in need. His kind, chatty coworker Daniel is dealing with an abusive boyfriend—something Wes, whose father was an alcoholic, has experience handling. Wes steps up to help Daniel kick his boyfriend to the curb, but in the process, he finds himself falling for Daniel himself.

Navigating a new relationship when they both have traumatic pasts is one thing. But when a shady group starts targeting the tiger they are trying to find a zoo placement for, the stakes are raised even higher. Can Wes and Daniel come together to rescue the animals—and each other?

SCAN THE QR CODE
BELOW TO PREORDER!